CHAMPAK

Started in 1969, Champak is the largest-selling children's magazine in India. Published in eight languages and reaching over six million kids, it's an inseparable part of childhood memories for most Indians. Champak's stories are beautifully illustrated, expand creativity and imagination, hone reading skills and bring positive self-worth. Through its stories, Champak encourages children to treat others with respect, kindness and sensitivity, helps develop cognitive and reasoning skills, and brings humour that is essential to a child's everyday life.

Published by
Rupa Publications India Pvt. Ltd 2025
7/16, Ansari Road, Daryaganj
New Delhi 110002

Sales centres:
Bengaluru Chennai
Hyderabad Jaipur Kathmandu
Kolkata Mumbai Prayagraj

Copyright © Delhi Press Patra Prakashan Pvt. Ltd., 2025

All rights reserved.
No part of this publication may be reproduced, transmitted, or stored in a retrieval system, in any form or by any means, electronic, mechanical, photocopying, recording or otherwise, without the prior permission of the publisher.

P-ISBN: 978-93-6156-634-9
E-ISBN: 978-93-6156-001-9

First impression 2025

10 9 8 7 6 5 4 3 2 1

Printed in India

This book is sold subject to the condition that it shall not, by way of trade or otherwise, be lent, resold, hired out, or otherwise circulated, without the publisher's prior consent, in any form of binding or cover other than that in which it is published.

CHAMPAK
Science
STORIES

RUPA

Kalpana Chawla loved reading Champak as a child. In 1997, she carried a T-Shirt with Champak logo to space on the space shuttle Columbia. She flew among the stars and inspires young minds to dream.

The Champak T-shirt that went to space
with Kalpana Chawla,
now proudly displayed at the Champak office.

Table of Contents

A NEW STAR IN THE SKY 05

A BRIGHT INVENTOR 11

CAN HUMANS FLY? 16

THE KITE DRONE 20

CAN YOU STEAL THE MOON? 26

THE MIRACLE VACCINE 30

LINU'S MARVELLOUS INVENTION 34

WEIGHING THE DONKEY 40

THE STRENGTH OF THE EARTH 46

THE THOUGHT MACHINE 51

THE STORY OF SIR HUMPHRY DAVY 57

A PAPERY JOURNEY 61

SLURPY THE SURVIVOR 66

THE BURJ ICE-SCRAPER 72

THE GIFT OF BRAILLE 78

A FIGHT OVER COLOURS................................ 84

WHO MADE THE MODEL? 92

VISITING TELEPHONE CITY 88

THE HAUNTED ROOM 95

SAHIL LEARNS BIRDWATCHING 98

BLOWING TO AND FRO 100

THE CAT IN THE COMPUTER....................... 105

Persona

Humour

Science

Nature

Medicine

A New Star in the Sky

By Kusum Agrawal

In Karnal, Haryana, a couple entered the Office of the Principal of Tagore Bal Niketan School. They had come for their daughter's admission and held her hand as they walked in. At the office, the Principal asked, "What's the child's father's name?"

"Madam, my name is Banarasi Lal Chawla," the father replied.

He gestured to his wife and said, "This is Sanjyoti, her mother."

The Principal looked at the child and asked her affectionately, "What's your name, dear?"

"Manto," said the little girl.

"That's your nickname, isn't it?" the Principal smiled, "What name should we use at school?"

The girl's mother said, "Madam, we've thought of three or four names. However, we haven't finalised one yet." She then told the Principal the names they had thought of.

Manto gets a new name

When she heard the names, Manto said at once, "Kalpana! I like the name Kalpana. May I have that name, please?"

"Why do you like the name Kalpana?" asked the Principal.

'Kalpana' means **imagination.** And I like to imagine and dream," said Manto.

The little girl had made up her mind and was enrolled in the school under the name "Kalpana."

"What is Kalpana's date of birth?" asked the Principal.

Her father and mother looked at each other and said hesitantly, "July 1, 1961."

Manto's actual date of birth was March 17, 1962. If they had told the Principal her exact date of birth, she would have been denied **ADMISSION**, as she was a year younger than the required age.

Manto was the youngest of their four children, but she was smart, and her parents felt she could start school right away. Kalpana's parents wanted their daughter admitted in this school because it was close to their home.

The admission process went smoothly, and soon, Kalpana started attending school. She was good at studies and began excelling in class.

One day, Kalpana returned home from school and said, "Mother, today all the children in school drew the map of India on the floor and painted it. It was a project, and everyone took part.

"Then you must have taken part too!" said her Mom.

"No, I didn't. Instead, I decorated the classroom's ceiling with black chart paper, painted bright dots on it, and made it look like outer space!"

Her mother knew that Kalpana was interested in space. She often saw Kalpana lie under the open sky and stare at the stars for hours.

Indian Women Astronauts-A Null Set

Time passed, and Kalpana reached class 10. It was the Mathematics period, and while explaining the null-set concept in **Algebra**, the teacher said, "A null set is also referred to as the empty set. It is a set that contains no elements. For example, let's say we have to find a set of all senior citizens who are less than five years old. There are no senior citizens under five, and a person has to be much older than five to be considered a senior citizen, isn't it? Thus, it is a null or an empty set. Let me give you another example. 'Indian Women ASTRONAUTS' – is a null set. That's because no Indian woman astronaut has gone into space!"

Sitting in the classroom, Kalpana said, "Maybe in a few years, someone will, and then it will no longer be an example of a null set."

The other students looked at her in surprise. But what she said was perhaps going to become true.

Soon, it was time for her to take admission for higher studies at college. Everyone was wondering what subject they should take up.

"I will pursue Engineering," announced Kalpana to her parents.

"No, no. You should become a doctor or a teacher. That's more suitable for girls," said her father.

Her mother was also of the same opinion, but Kalpana did not budge. She insisted until her parents gave in, and Kalpana secured admission at Chandigarh Engineering College.

When she chose to pursue **AERONAUTICAL ENGINEERING**, her teachers said, "This branch is not for girls. There won't be a single girl in your class except you. You'll have to study alone."

"I don't care," said Kalpana. "I'll study alone if I have to." Kalpana studied and completed aeronautical engineering, much to the surprise of **naysayers**. She proved to her family and country that a girl could become an aeronautical engineer. After completing the course, Kalpana wanted to study further. She was an unstoppable force; nobody dared get in her way, and she kept going till she reached space.

Kalpana-The First Indian woman in Space

The world now knows her as Kalpana Chawla—the first Indian woman to go to Space!

After completing aeronautical engineering in 1982, she went to the United States and pursued a degree in aerospace engineering at the University of Texas, graduating in 1984. In 1988, NASA selected her, where she underwent training for the next 7 years. In 1995, Kalpana Chawla took her first space flight. On November 19, 1997, on board the STS-87 Columbia Shuttle, she spent 372 hours in space and returned to Earth on December 5, 1997.

Kalpana went again to space for the second time on January 16, 2003, on the space shuttle 'Columbia'. It was a 16- day project. Kalpana Chawla and six colleagues stayed in space, researched, and gathered data. On entering the Earth's **atmosphere** on February 1, 2003, the Columbia **space shuttle** burst into flames and crashed over Texas, USA. Kalpana Chawla and her six colleagues lost their lives.

Kalpana Chawla is no longer with us, but the dream she pursued proved that girls are in no way less than anyone. She said that she was meant to go into space and that she was meant to die there, too. She completed her **MISSION** before bidding farewell to the world. Since then, a new star has shone bright and bold in the inky black sky, encouraging little Mantos everywhere to 'reach for the stars'.

PUZZLE TIME

MEMORY

February 11 is Inventors' Day. NASA invented MOXIE, a device attached to the Mars Perseverance Rover that helps separate oxygen from the air.

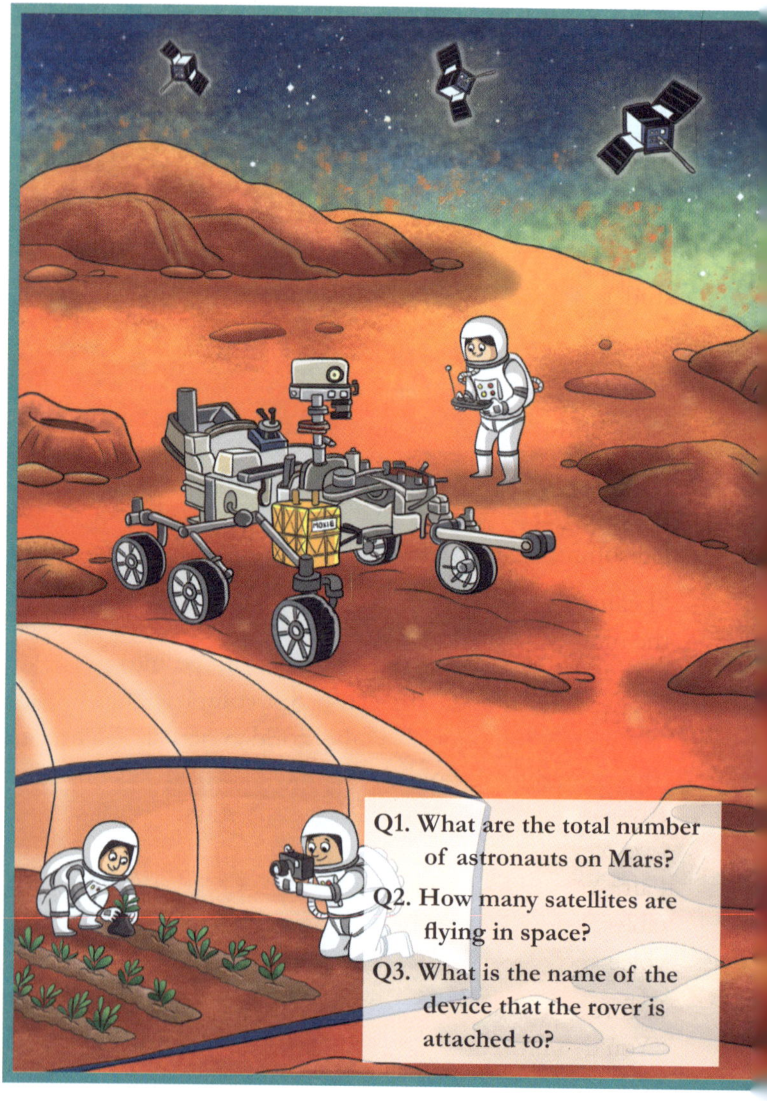

Q1. What are the total number of astronauts on Mars?

Q2. How many satellites are flying in space?

Q3. What is the name of the device that the rover is attached to?

A Bright Inventor
By Harbans Singh

Thomas Alva Edison was a great American **inventor** and businessman. One of his most significant inventions was the electric bulb.

This story takes us back to when Edison was a primary school student.

His classmate Wilson, who sat beside him asked, "Are you new to this city?"

"Yes, we have recently come to Michigan state from Ohio," Edison replied.

"You seem a little weak and sick," Wilson said, scanning Edison from head to toe.

"I came down with a high fever and severe throat irritation the moment I arrived in this city. The doctor said it was **scarlet fever**. I also have trouble hearing with my left ear," Edison admitted in all earnestness.

The Harsh Teacher

Alva did not notice that his class teacher was watching the two of them chatting. "Have you come to a classroom or a Fair? Yesterday, I made you **MEMORISE** the 13-times tables. Stand up and recite them! Quick!" The teacher's loud voice and blazing eyes made Edison tremble.

Before he could collect himself, the teacher shouted again, "You don't remember, do you? Come here and try to recite a

poem from your English book. I am sure you won't be able to do that either. You are a DISTRACTED boy!"

Poor Edison forgot even what he already knew. Dejected, he stared at the floor.

The next day, the teacher gave Edison a sealed envelope and said, "Give this to your parents without fail."

Edison's mother was in the backyard, hanging up washed clothes to dry. Edison tugged on her dress and gave her the **envelope**. His mother went inside the house and sat on a **wooden** chair to read the letter.

Young Edison's eyes were on her, as she read the letter, tears welling up in the corners of her eyes.

Mother knows best

The teacher had made insensitive remarks about Edison in the letter.

It read, 'Your child is mentally weak. Kindly do not send him to school. Try to educate him at home.'

Edison's mother was a Dutch woman named Nancy Matthew Elliot. She folded up the letter after she was finished reading it, and **kissed** Edison's little head. Lifting him into her lap, she smiled and said, "Son, your teacher has written that you are very intelligent and the school is not good enough for you. The teachers there are not very bright and therefore can't teach you much. So, you will be **home-schooled**, and isn't that going to be fun!"

"Alright, mother! From now on, I will study with you!" Edison was delighted.

His mother put the envelope in a bag and kept it high up in a cupboard, out of Edison's reach.

A few years later, Edison's mother bought him a book that had many **experiments** described in it. Edison's home was already his school and he enjoyed performing the experiments from the book in the comfort of his house, in a spare room that he had rigged up into a lab.

"Son, where did you get the equipment for the laboratory from? You certainly didn't ask me for money to buy it!" his mother asked.

"I spent all my pocket money on setting up the laboratory."

"Alright, son, but you have started spending too much time in the You've been forgetting your meals!." Edison nodded and went back into his lab.

Edison makes Progress

When he was 14 years old, Edison saved a 3-year-old child's life at the railway station. The child's father thanked Edison and in return, trained him later to operate the telegram machine as a job-skill.

Edison got a job as a TELEGRAM machine operator at the railway station. He worked nights, so he could spend the daytime in his laboratory.

Edison made all his important discoveries and inventions from 1879 to 1900. By that time, he had become a rich businessman but never stopped being an inventor. There were 1093 patents in his name at that time!

One day, he was looking for some important papers when he found his mother's old bag which contained his schoolteacher's letter .

He pulled the letter out of the ENVELOPE and read it. Memories flashed like scenes from a movie. For a brief moment, he felt angry. He read it again, and stood before his mother's PHOTOGRAPH, tears streaming from his eyes. His mother had passed away without so much as a whisper about this letter to him.

"Mother, if you had read this letter to me as it was written, if you had scolded me saying I was stupid and useless, I would have broken. I would not have become the successful person that I am today. You changed my life, Mother."

Lightbulb Moment

In September 1882, 40 electric BULBS made by Thomas Alva Edison were going to be lit at a public event. Around 3000 people had assembled at the Pearl Street Power Station which was being inaugurated with this attraction. $40,000 was invested  to create Edison's bulbs and a lot was at stake. Everything went SWIMMINGLY well, and Edison's bulbs were appreciated and applauded.

That day he said, "Before creating these 40 bulbs, I conducted 10,000 experiments, faced financial challenges and accepted COUNTLESS failures. But success requires hard work and perseverance, and that is what has led me here today."

The rest, of course, is history. The electric bulb reached and lit up every corner of the world, enabling people to work even during the night.

Thomas Alva Edison passed away on October 18, 1931, but his legacy lives on, in the form of lightbulbs in every office, home, cafe and street.

Can Humans Fly?

By Rajeev Gupta

Sunny, Marty and Coco were playing on the branches of a tree when suddenly, an AEROPLANE whooshed through the sky above them. They had never seen an aeroplane before and were quite surprised and alarmed at the same time.

"Mom, look! There's a huge bird flying across the sky!" Sunny called out to their mother.

"Yes, Mom! It's very big and is making a loud noise," added Marty.

"It is so shiny, unlike any bird I have seen!" exclaimed Coco.

Mini, their mother, laughed and explained, "That is not a bird. It's an aeroplane. Humans use it to reach far-off places in a short time."

"Wow! Humans can fly?" asked Marty, surprised.

"But I have never seen any human with wings," said Coco.

"They do not have wings, but can build machines that do. The machines are called 'aeroplanes', and all they have

to do is sit inside one. The aeroplane will take them from one place to another," said Mini.

The Concept of Flying Humans

"Mom, how did they build this aeroplane?," asked Sunny.

"Humans came up with the idea of flying when they saw us flying," said Mini, "They thought it would be a faster way to cover long distances."

"When did they build their first aeroplane?" asked Coco.

"The first aeroplane was not built in one go. The one that you saw today is the result of many scientists working over several **decades** on different designs. In fact, people have been attempting to fly or build flying devices since **ancient** times," explained Mini.

"So, there were other designs?" Marty asked.

"Yes, Marty. Do you remember the time we flew past the park last week?" asked Mini, "I showed you a lot of people flying **paper kites**."

"Yes, Mom," said Coco. "Sunny and Marty thought they were sky-fishes," she laughed. .

"Paper kites are one of the earliest man-made **FLYING OBJECTS**. People in China designed them hundreds of years ago. Some kites were so big that they could even carry a human with them," said Mini.

Her children listened in awe. "Later, humans discovered that they could fill balloons with a gas called **HYDROGEN** to make them float up and fly," Mini added.

"But Mom, even balloons that they merely blow air into, can fly. Then why do they use hydrogen?" asked Sunny.

"These are special balloons that are really big in order to carry humans in them," said Mini, "In 1783, two brothers, Orville and Wilbur, used hydrogen-filled balloons to lift themselves into the sky. They became known as the 'Wright Brothers', and people consider them the **PIONEERS** of air-travel. Once, a goat was attached to one such balloon and sent into the air!" said Mini.

Her children giggled at the thought of a **BLEATING** goat being carried by a large balloon into the sky.

"It's true," said Mini, "Haven't you heard Uncle Lonu saying that it was his great-grandfather who was sent up in that balloon?"

The Big Shiny Machine

"How did humans change the design from a balloon to the big shiny machine we just saw?" asked Marty.

"Ah, we helped humans achieve this," trilled Mini, her chest puffing up, "They understood that our tails and wings help us fly and maintain our balance in the air. Inspired by us, they designed a machine with wings and a tail!" replied Mini.

"Mom, our wings don't just help us to fly straight. We can dip, dive, swoop, lift off and do so much more! Can an aeroplane do that too?" asked Sunny.

Mini laughed, "Yes, the Wright Brothers dreamt of building a powerful machine that could fly and also be controlled by a human. They call that human a 'Pilot'. The **PILOT** sits in a small unit at the front of the aeroplane, and has at his **DISPOSAL**, a variety of buttons and controls to **manoeuvre** the aeroplane."

"They must have been delighted with their success, right Mom?" asked Coco.

"Yes, dear," Mini replied, "Humans are usually very happy with their successes. Everything they build or invent, makes their lives easier."

"Mom, how many humans can an aeroplane carry?" asked Marty.

"They make them in different sizes," Mini informed Marty, "The smallest ones carry just two people, but the bigger ones, like the aeroplane you just saw, can carry even 500 humans. And these machines can travel pretty fast," said Mini, "Some of them are much faster than us!"

"I bet I can beat that aeroplane if I tried!" said Coco, **FLAPPING** her tiny wings.

Mini laughed, "Aeroplanes have a tank which gets filled with a liquid called **AVIATION GASOLINE**. This makes them fly faster. If you want to catch up, you'd better eat well and grow stronger!"

The Kite Drone

By Amitabh Shankar Roy Chaudhary

Toto Goes Missing

For months, tigers had been vanishing from the Sariska forest, leaving all the animals worried and wondering what had happened to them.

One day, Bagga the tiger, King of Sariska, ANNOUNCED "Whoever helps find the missing tigers will be generously rewarded."

It was Makar Sankranti, and that same day, during Makar Sankranti, when children gathered by the Sariska lake to fly their kites, Rambo, the father of Toto tiger, came running and crying, "My Toto hasn't come home since last night! I've searched everywhere, but I can't find him. Please help!"

The animals were filled with worry. What could they do? Peacocks began flying around to **SEARCH**, and several of Toto's bear friends climbed trees to look from higher ground. But after a while, they returned with disappointed faces, saying, "Uncle, we couldn't spot him anywhere. The forest is too dense to see very far."

Chanchal the rabbit had been silently observing. He stepped forward and said, "I have an idea. This **Makar Sankranti**, my dad gave me a very light mobile phone with an excellent **camera**. What if we use it to search the forest?"

Toteram the parrot, perched on a branch, scoffed, "What will you do with that phone? Fly around the whole forest holding it?"

"Just wait and see," Chanchal replied. He dashed into his nest and quickly came out with two large **kites**, two spools of thread, and his phone. Handing one kite to his friend Balloo the bear, he explained, "You'll fly one kite, and I'll fly the other. We'll attach the phone between them. Once it's up, the phone can take photos every 30 seconds in auto-mode, so we can **scan** the forest from above."

"Will the kites be able to bear the weight of the phone?" Balloo asked, doubtful.

"Don't worry," Chanchal assured him, "The phone is super light, the kites are top-quality, and everyone knows you're the best kite-flier around."

"But how far up will we fly the kites?" Balloo wondered.

"We'll keep them close enough to capture images of the forest floor," Chanchal explained.

The Kite Drone works!

Chanchal's plan was set into motion. Bittu and Chikki, two squirrels, climbed a tree with the kites. Chanchal told them to adjust the phone's settings so it would take photos for twenty whole minutes. Then, Chanchal and Balloo each climbed separate trees, standing opposite each other. Bittu and Chikki **secured** the phone tightly between the two kites and handed them over.

Once everything was in place, Chanchal gave the signal, and the kites took flight. The squirrels scampered down, and all the animals of Sariska watched in awe. A gentle breeze began to blow, **lifting** the kites higher, carrying the phone with ease.

Totaram parrot, excited, started flapping his wings and shouting, "Look at that! Chanchal has turned a kite into a DRONE! Bravo!"

For a while, Chanchal and Balloo manoeuvred the kites, capturing photos across the forest. They pulled the strings tight, then let them loose, flying the kites over different areas.

Eventually, Balloo called out, "Chanchal, we need to bring them down before the phone battery dies out."

"Good point," Chanchal replied. "Let's lower the kite drone carefully."

After bringing the kites down, Chanchal eagerly checked the photos. Balloo and the other animals gathered around, while Bittu and Chikki jumped up to peek at the screen.

Chanchal exclaimed, "Look at this! Someone has dug a PIT, and Toto's fallen into it!"

"Who would do such a thing?" Chikki asked angrily.

"This is the work of poachers," said Ela the eagle, spreading her wings.

"We'll deal with them," declared Richpal the bear, the forest inspector. "Let me take a closer look at the scene." The animals were furious and wanted to rush to Toto's aid,

but Richpal cautioned them. "We need to be smart about this. If we go as a group, the poachers will get away. I'll take my team and hide near the pit, and when they return, we'll catch them."

Rambo pleaded, "Please, save my son!"

"Don't worry, Rambo," Bagga reassured him. "We'll get Toto and also make sure this never happens again."

Catching the Poachers

Before nightfall, the poachers returned to the pit in a jeep. Richpal's team was waiting. As soon as the poachers stepped out, the animals sprang into action, **capturing** them before they could escape. Richpal arrested the poachers, and Toto was rescued from the pit.

Rambo rushed to hug his son, tears in his eyes.

King Bagga **rewarded** Chanchal for his bravery, and gifted him a large field of grass.

Chanchal said, "Your Majesty, everyone helped save Toto. Let's make the field open to all, so anyone in need can always find food there."

Balloo, Bittu, and Chikki **EMBRACED** Chanchal and said, "Our friend Chanchal isn't just the smartest; he's also the kindest, always ready to help!"

COLOUR ME

PUZZLE TIME

CAN YOU STEAL THE MOON?

By Gyandev Mukesh

The Superintendent of Black Forest Police Station, Hetu the fox, was not displaying the right conduct for a **POLICEMAN**. Everybody in the jungle was upset with his behaviour.

A Wrongful Accusation

One evening Hetu, along with a few other policemen, was patrolling the jungle. It was becoming dark and the moon had started rising. Superintendent Hetu saw Nikko the squirrel, **GAZING** at the moon. He approached Nikko and asked, "Why are you looking at the moon like you're planning to steal it?"

Nikko got scared and pleaded, "Sir, the moon cannot be stolen. It is so high up in the sky. I couldn't reach it even if I tried." Hetu wanted to trap Nikko, so he said, "All I know

is that your **INTENTION** was to steal the moon. I've caught you. You will be punished for it."

Poor Nikko was arrested and taken to jail. Blacky the bear was the Judge of the jungle. He was like Hetu too, and did not care much about Law and Order.

On the day Nikko's case was being heard, all the animals gathered in Blacky's **courtroom**. Lawyer Alok the elephant was representing Nikko.

Nikko's Desperation

Judge Blacky said, "What do you have to say in your defence, Nikko?" Nikko said, "Sir, the sun, moon and stars are elements of nature. They cannot be stolen. I am not a thief." The animals listened as he continued, "The moon is a satellite that revolves around the earth. The sunlight that falls on it is reflected off its surface and reaches the earth. How can I try to steal such a powerful object?"

"The **intention** to steal is what counts. One who has such a desire, will sooner or later hatch a plan and carry it out. You will be punished for your intention to steal, for sure." Blacky banged his hammer on the table.

Lawyer Alok brought forth his best **arguments** and tried convincing Judge Blacky, but he was obstinate and refused to change his **judgement**.

A Clever Tactic

Finally Lawyer Alok stood up and said, "Sir, you are right. The offence starts with the thought. Nikko intended to steal and that is why he deserves to be punished. Since this is a **PECULIAR** case, the **PUNISHMENT** should also be unique." Judge Blacky said, "What do you mean?" Lawyer Alok said, "Please give me the opportunity to decide on a punishment for him. I will suggest a suitable one that will set an example in this jungle." Judge Blacky said, "Alright, you may decide the punishment on my behalf, but it had better be a strong one."

Alok said, "Sir, he wished to steal a rare marvel like the moon. So, he should be taken to the moon and left there."

Judge Blacky and Officer Hetu were aghast. "Nonsense! How can we take him to the moon? No one can reach there. No staircase, rope or bridge, no matter how long or high, can reach the moon from the earth," Blacky said.

Justice is Served

"Aha!" Alok picked up their point, "Sirs, you are absolutely right. When it is impossible for us to reach the moon, how can anyone even think of stealing it?"

Blacky and Hetu were now in a spot. They said, "No, he has to be punished, as he was looking at the moon with the desire to steal

it." Alok the elephant said, "Alright then, Sir. Once the police department is ready with a mode of **TRANSPORT**, we will **BANISH** Nikko to the moon."

The Judge and the Police Superintendent knew that they had been beaten. All charges against Nikko had to be dropped. That day Hetu and Blacky got booed so much by everyone in the courtroom that they decided to change their ways for the better.

THE MIRACLE VACCINE

By Sudha Goswami

After the school bell rang that afternoon, 8-year-old Ruchi walked hastily towards the bus-stop. Her friend, Trisha accompanied her. The walk home, once they got off the bus, was going to be a bit long.

Ruchi's mother had asked her to come home as early as she could, as they had to take Ruchi's baby brother, Jay, to the nearest Clinic to get him a dose of the Polio Vaccine. Jay was 3-and-a-half years old. Every year, a **polio vaccination** campaign was held in their city to vaccinate all the children, up to the age of five. Ruchi's parents were well aware of the dangers of Polio. The risk of not vaccinating children was that they stood the risk of being affected by the **DREADED** disease, if they weren't. Ruchi had been given the vaccine when she was younger.

Ruchi learns about Polio

Ruchi's father had told her, "Polio is an infection that enters the body through the mouth or nose and spreads to the throat and intestines. It reaches other organs and affects the central nervous system - the spine and brain."

"This disease is called '**Poliomyelitis**' or 'infant stroke' and can cause **disability** and death in children," he had told her, "The polio **VIRUS** spreads from person to person and attacks the brain and spinal cord. The affected person's arms and legs stop functioning. It can even cause paralysis! Although India has been declared polio-free for seven or eight years now, countries like Pakistan, Afghanistan and Nigeria are not yet free of it."

Ruchi had gone to the clinic the previous year with her neighbour, Aunty Ratna. There she saw the saliva and stool samples of children being tested. If a child was severely infected, a fluid was collected from the top or bottom of their spine and sent for testing.

Upon Aunty Ratna's query at the clinic, the Doctor had said, "25% of the children show up with a fever, sore throat, nausea, headache, fatigue or body ache. A more severe symptom is

'Paresthesia', which causes their hands and feet to feel as if pins and needles are pricking into them. This could lead to **'Meningitis',** an infection of the brain and the spinal cord, which causes paralysis or an inability to move the arms and legs. It puts strain on the lung muscles used for breathing."

What is a Virologist?

When Ruchi had returned from the clinic that day, her mother had more to say. "The World Health Organization is striving to wipe out polio," she had told Ruchi, "World Polio Day is celebrated worldwide every year on October 24, as that was the birthday of Jonas Salk, the American virologist who developed the polio vaccine in 1952."

"What is a Virologist, Ma?" Ruchi had asked.

"A scientist who studies and figures out ways to fight viruses, my dear", her mother had told her, "He created the first ever polio vaccine. It was introduced to the world on April 12, 1955 and was made from a dose of **inactivated** or dead polioviruses." Ruchi's father had told her, "An oral vaccine was also developed by Albert Sabin using weakened polioviruses. Trials began in 1957, and a **LICENSE** for production was granted in 1962."

Ruchi and Jay get a Treat!

Ruchi kept going back to her parents with more questions and found out that the Global Polio **Eradication** Initiative was established in 1988. The World Health Organization and Rotary International were determined to stamp out polio globally. **Vaccination** prevents the disease entirely! Just two drops of the vaccine had saved millions of people from the deadly disease, and continues to do so.

Ruchi made it home on time and her brother Jay was taken to the Clinic to get his polio vaccination. They returned home, assured that Jay would stay protected from Polio for the rest of his life. On the way home, Ruchi's mother bought them chocolate **pastries**, making it a memorable day for Ruchi and Jay.

Linu's Marvellous Invention

By Ilika Priya

Linu the honeybee was an intelligent student. She loved science. After her class X exams, she enrolled to study science in class XI.

On the first day of class, she flew **ENTHUSIASTICALLY** into the science laboratory where she met Shantu the horse, Wini the deer and Chuchu the cat. They were conducting **EXPERIMENTS** with test tubes and chemicals. Linu immediately wanted to grab a test tube.

"Linu, this is not for you. You are tinier than the test tube. It won't fit in your hands. You won't be able to lift it," warned Shantu. Linu drifted off towards a beaker of chemicals.

"This is not meant for you either. You will find it too heavy," said Wini.

Linu was upset. Nobody was letting her touch anything in the laboratory. Teary-eyed, she flew out. "Everyone is making fun of me because I'm tiny. One day I'll prove them wrong," she decided.

Linu begins inventing

Linu reached home, pulled out a few science books, and began reading them in detail.

"I have found many interesting things to do!" said Linu, slamming the book shut after she had read it. She worked hard, conducting new experiments everyday. She studied **NANOTECHNOLOGY** with great interest and even invented a few nanodevices for herself.

Nanotechnology is the science of manipulating materials on an atomic or molecular scale, especially to build microscopic devices.

"Now since my equipment is tiny, like me, conducting experiments will be simpler," thought Linu, as she made a small **SCIENCE KIT** for herself.

Linu spent days and nights inventing new things. One day she poured some liquid from her test tube on an ant and it shrunk so much that she could hardly see it with her naked eye.

Linu jumped with joy. "Wow! I did it! I can reduce the size of anything using this liquid." She put the liquid in a bottle and flew out of her house **TRIUMPHANTLY.**

After returning, Linu picked up the bottle and sprinkled a drop of her invention on herself. Lo behold - she became tinier!

Linu looked at herself in a mirror and found that her wings had become much smaller. She had become so tiny that she could hide inside a CALCULATOR.

Linu gets too Excited

Linu couldn't hold herself back and flew right back to the science laboratory and into a calculator. The parts inside the calculator seemed too big. She placed her foot on a button on the calculator and the corresponding number appeared on the screen.

She flew out of the calculator and found herself in a computer class. Someone had brought the calculator into the class. She saw that the students were working away on computers.

She flew onto Lily the sparrow's computer and started pressing some keys on her keyboard.

"What is wrong with my computer?" wondered Lily. "How are these letters appearing on the screen AUTOMATICALLY?"

She summoned the attention of the other students and all of them peered at her computer.

"I think there is a virus in Lily's computer," said Tinku the panther. Suddenly Lily's computer stopped MALFUNCTIONING and the same started in Ranu the squirrel's computer. Frightened, Ranu ran out of the lab. There was a lot of commotion and computer experts were called in to correct the problem. The experts found nothing wrong with the systems, and began to reboot all of them. Linu flew out of the computer class and back towards the science laboratory.

"Students, look! There is PHOSPHORUS in this test-tube. It catches fire when coming into contact with even a drop of water or too much moisture in the air. We need to be careful while working with it," their science teacher Weme the GOAT was saying as she placed the test-tube in its stand. Without warning, the test-tube exploded, shocking the students and Weme.

A Knock-out Realisation

"Strange things have been happening at our school," said Weme worriedly, "Letters appear **AUTOMATICALLY** on the computer screen; test-tubes are exploding on their own and now look at the colour of the chemical in the test-tube. It has turned red!"

Linu was overjoyed, "Now I can do whatever I want. I am so tiny that no one can see or stop me." She flew towards the regulator of the ceiling fan and got inside it. She then touched the switch-port of the regulator.

"Ouch!" Linu got an electric shock and was flung away. Thankfully the current was not too strong. She **SHOOK** herself up and flew out of the **REGULATOR**. Sitting in a corner of the room, Linu began to breathe heavily. She realised that she had gotten carried away.

"Pride goes before a fall, and yet we let it go right to our heads. It's good that I realised my mistake, else I would have had to pay a big price," she thought to herself.

But Linu was now growing bigger! The nano **CONSTRICTIONS** were getting disrupted due to the electric current. In a few minutes, she came back to her original size."Linu!" everyone exclaimed. Linu narrated all that had happened to the class. "Sorry, Linu. We belittled you, and you felt insulted," said Wini the fawn.

"I agree that you hurt me, but that doesn't justify my misuse of science. I became too proud, disturbed everyone and hurt myself in the process. I have now realised my mistake. I'm sorry!" Linu bowed her head.

"You could demonstrate your inventions in class and teach everyone a thing or two, Linu!" said their teacher Weme. Linu was the most excited that she had ever been in the longest time, and hummed happily as she flew home to start preparing.

MAP QUEST

PUZZLE TIME

Radha is at her school's science lab and she needs to find the right combination of chemicals to perform her experiment. Find out which table has the right combination of chemicals and equipment with the help of the clues given:

1. Radha needs a red-coloured chemical and a blue coloured chemical to perform her experiment.
2. She needs two test tubes for the experiment.
3. The chemical bottles have glass stoppers on them.

Weighing the Donkey

By Omprakash Kshatriya

"Can you tell me how much this donkey weighs?" asked Mr. Yadav, the science teacher, to his students at a picnic.

"Who can tell me exactly how much this animal weighs?" he asked again, pointing at a donkey GRAZING in a nearby field.

All the students looked at each other as they could not figure out how anything could be weighed without a weighing scale.

"You have five minutes to think," said Mr Yadav.

They were standing on a RIVERBANK, and the soil was black. The field's BOUNDARY was covered with grass, and a pile of stones was stacked near the field.

Tango Footprint

Suddenly, Reena exclaimed, "Sir, I know its weight!"

She removed a metal ruler from her backpack and said, "I can tell the APPROXIMATE weight of the donkey." She went closer to the donkey and bent to see its muddy feet.

Mr. Yadav cautioned, "Don't stand behind the donkey. It may kick you in **DEFENCE**. It is called a '**MULE-KICK**'." The students started laughing. They found the idea of a 'mule-kick' amusing. "And if it kicks you, it'll knock all your teeth out," said Mohit.

Amar said, "Let's make Ramesh stand behind the donkey. He likes to be mule-kicked. Ho-ho!"

Reena did not want to get a mule-kick. She held the ruler in front of the donkey. The donkey became wary and took a couple of steps back.

Reena looked down at the damp soil on which the donkey was standing. It's feet had sunk in and left footprints. Reena bent and measured their depth.

Then, she made her **FOOTPRINT**'s in the soil and measured their depth too.

She compared the depths of both the footprints, made some calculations mentally and said, "The depth of this donkey's footprints is five times that of mine. So, it weighs five times as much as I do. My weight is 38 kilograms. Five times 38 is 190, So the donkey weighs 190 kilograms."

All the students clapped in awe. They thought she had correctly guessed the donkey's weight.

"Well done, Reena! Your way of estimating it is **logical** and you may be near its weight. However, I want the exact weight of the Donkey. Who can find that out?" asked Mr. Yadav.

Climbing on the Donkey

Ramesh grabbed the chance and quickly said, "Sir, I'll tell you the exact weight," he winked at his friends. They figured out he was up to some mischief. Ramesh, along with his four friends, walked closer to the donkey. Ramesh signalled his friends and said, "Sit on this donkey one by one. I'll hold its rope."

First, Amar sat on the donkey, followed by Rahul. But when Jitu sat on it, the donkey started braying loudly. "Heee-haw, Hee-Haw!" The students were startled. Ramesh said, "Sir, the donkey is asking us to stop. If even one more student sits on it, it will tumble down."

"That's interesting," laughed Mr. Yadav, "So, now you know donkey-language!"

The students laughed, and Ramesh blushed, his cheeks pink. He pointed at Gita, who was a bit skinny, and asked, "Will you please sit on the donkey?"

When Gita came towards it, the donkey brayed loudly once more. When she sat on it, the donkey began to bray much louder. Immediately, Ramesh helped Gita get off its back. "The rest of you, please get down as well!" Ramesh looked at Amar, Rahul and Jitu and started adding their weights.. "Sir, this donkey weighs 162 kilograms,"
Ramesh announced.

Mr. Yadav asked him, "How did you **DERIVE** that answer?"

Ramesh replied, "Sir, when Amar, Rahul and Jitu sat on the donkey, it was **BRAYING** as it had too much weight on its back. But when Gita sat on it, it started braying much louder as if to say it could not hold any more weight. So, its weight equals that of Amar, Rahul and Jitu."

"And how do you know the weight of these three students?"

"Sir, you measured everyone's height and weight on the way to the picnic. So, I remembered my friends' weights," replied Ramesh. "Oh! You have a sharp memory!" praised Mr. Yadav, "You have estimated the donkey's weight, but you could be mistaken. Often, a 40-kilogram person can lift 80 kilograms of weight. You must have seen porters who carry bags at railway stations who carry weights much heavier than theirs." "Yes, Sir, you are right," said Ramesh disappointed. Mr. Yadav looked at the other students and asked, "Now, who will attempt to tell me its exact weight?" Vikas, who had been silent thus far, said, "Sir, I can tell!"

"Come forward, Vikas! You are welcome to try."

The Donkey Stands on the Boat

Vikas called out to the the donkey's master, who was nearby, watching all this. With the master's PERMISSION and help, he took the donkey to a boat and made the donkey climb into it. The boat sank a little as soon as the donkey stood on it. Vikas marked the water level up to which the boat had sunk.

"When the donkey boarded the boat, it sank till here," he pointed. Then, with the master's help, he got the donkey out of the boat.

Vikas called out to two of his friends, "Please climb into the boat."

His friends clambered into the boat, and after they sat down, the boat sank into the water with their weight. Vikas examined whether the boat had sunk up to the mark that had been set by the donkey. It had'nt. Seeing this, Vikas asked Gita to get into the boat as well. Vikas looked at the donkey's mark, which was still slightly above.

"Reena! Could you please bring me a few one-kilogram packs of ghee and oil?" Reena ran towards the camp and brought an armload of ghee packets. Vikas placed them in the boat one by one. As soon as the water touched the 'donkey's weight' mark on the boat, he stopped and shouted excitedly, "Sir, the donkey weighs as much as the total of all of the weights in the boat." He added their weights.

Eureka moment!

"The exact weight of this donkey is 182 kilograms," said Vikas with a smile. "Well done, Vikas! You calculated the exact weight of this donkey by using the 'Archimedes principle', which states that the donkey's weight is equal to the weight of the water it DISPLACES. The mark made on the boat when the donkey stood on it, indicated the donkey's weight. When the total weights of the three children and the ghee reached that mark, it meant their weight was the same as that of the donkey, according to the principle."

The students were thrilled that one of them had deducted the correct answer. They applauded Vikas, who was BEAMING with pride at having used a fundamental theorem to come up with a precise answer to such tricky question!

THE STRENGTH OF THE EARTH

By R. K. Vashisht

Monty the Monkey loved swing from one tree to another and was so skilled at it, that he could do it with his eyes closed. Monty's best friend Toto the tortoise could not even climb trees, let alone swinging from one to another. He tried to climb the tree on which Monty was sitting so that he too could enjoy the experience, but kept falling on his back with each attempt.

Monty saw that his friend was **distraught**. He climbed down from the tree and asked, "What's the matter, Toto?"

Toto answered, "I feel **USELESS**. I can't climb a tree."

Toto's Dilemma

"All of us are born with different talents. I can climb trees. Our friend Seetu the rhinoceros can't climb trees but can indeed uproot one. Different strokes for different folks!" Monty shrugged.

"That's fine, but I still think I have no talent," lamented Toto. "I have heard that you are the most intelligent student in your class, and that is something to be proud of!" Monty reminded Toto, "But tell me, why do you want to climb this tree?" "To eat mangoes," Toto said timidly. "Is that all?" Monty laughed and climbed the tree in a **jiffy**. He brought down two ripe mangoes. He gave one to Toto and said, "What are friends for, if not to help each other?"

Monty and Toto began regularly eating mangoes - Monty would pluck them from the branches and bring them down for both to share. One such day, when Monty was plucking mangoes atop a tree, he slipped and fell to the ground. Toto helped Monty and made him rest against the tree's trunk. Monty was in a lot of pain and fainted. When he opened his eyes, he saw Doctor Hiru the giraffe. Toto had brought him to Monty. Doctor Hiru examined him thoroughly. After giving Monty an **INJECTION** and some medicines, he left saying, "No broken bones, and that's good! Make sure he gets plenty of rest."

Why do we fall down?

Toto took good care of his friend. Within a few days, Monty was back to his healthy self. One day Monty asked, "Toto, why do we fall down?" Toto laughed and replied, "Would you rather fall upwards?"

"I mean - why do we fall at all? Even if we do, why can't we fall gently so that we don't get hurt?" "That's not possible Monty, because Earth has a **GRAVITATIONAL** force at its centre that pulls us towards it. That's why we fall downwards." Monty had a lot more questions about gravity as he didn't go to school. Toto however did, and presented all of Monty's questions to his teacher Elmo the elephant.

Elmo listened to all the questions carefully and said, "None of Monty's questions are wrong. If he was a student in our school, I would have been able to teach him all of this. However, there is another way to answer his questions." Toto asked eagerly, "What is that, Sir?"

Elmo replied, "I will take all of you on a short trip tomorrow. Bring Monty along."

Understanding Gravity

The next day Toto, his classmates, and Monty boarded the bus along with Elmo. The **destination** was a secret and eventually the bus stopped in front of a big building. Elmo showed a pass to the security guard who opened the gate and let them in. The building was round in shape and had a glass door through which the children peered in. They saw many strange and fascinating machines inside. They gasped when they saw Harry the hippopotamus floating around! He was wearing a thick white suit which was attached to some of the machines there, with long cables which also floated alongside him. Monty was thrilled. He had always

wanted to fly in the air, and what Harry was doing seemed very exciting.

Elmo said, "Children, this is Nandanvan's Space Centre. Scientist Harry the hippo is practising to be an astronaut! He is leaving for Space soon, aboard the space shuttle 'Nandanyaan'. He will conduct research there for three months." Monty said, "Sir, Harry is enjoying himself because he is in no danger of falling down. When I fell down from a tree the other day, I was badly hurt."

Staging Afloat

Elmo laughed and replied, "That's why I have brought you here - to show you why gravity is important. There is no gravity in Space. Similar conditions have been created in this lab so that Harry can get adjusted to zero-gravity. Gravity keeps your feet on the ground. It helps you walk,

run, jump, play - all of that. It is difficult to work without gravity." He added, "Think about it - when Harry tries to brush his teeth in Space, the toothpaste will float out of the tube! If he loses grip on any object, it will float away. Harry could get hurt by floating objects. In order to sleep, he will have to fasten himself to a bed using a belt. If he does not, he will float around and hurt himself by bumping against the walls!"

The children laughed, but Monty was listening in rapt attention. "Harry won't be able to have any of the tasty food that all of you eat everyday. He will have to eat special food that is bland but easily digestible. When he comes back, he will have to stay at the Nandanvan Hospital for some time to get re-adapted to the Earth's atmosphere."

Monty and the other children were **astonished** to hear this. Elmo continued, "You have no idea how much Harry is going to miss gravity! Let's wave to him and leave him to his training." As soon as Harry looked at them, Elmo and his students waved and cheered wildly. Harry responded with both thumbs-ups from inside his space suit. While leaving the Space Centre, Elmo walked with Monty, "Hope you're not angry with gravity any more, Monty!."

Monty said, "No, Sir. Our lives are possible only due to gravity. The right thing to do, is to be more aware and careful when we challenge it by climbing trees or running too fast." He paused for a second and added. "Sir, I also want to study, like Toto. Can I come to school from tomorrow?"

Elmo replied with delight, "Most certainly!"

THE THOUGHT MACHINE

By Debashish Majumdar

Sarita was surprised! Here she was, thinking of eating a cheese-and-onion **PIZZA** for lunch and there was Dad, coming in with a boxful of the treat!

"What a coincidence!" remarked Sarita, "This is exactly what I wanted to eat."

After lunch, Sarita visited a pet shop. She loved cats and this shop was full of them - thin cats, fat cats, **striped** cats and sleepy cats. She was attracted to a particularly **Cuddly** one with large blue **DROOPY** eyes.

"I wish I had enough pocket money to buy this cat," she thought.

Wishes come true

That evening Anita Aunty dropped in. She was visiting from

another city. Tucked in her arms was the same cuddly cat with droopy eyes Sarita had seen at the pet shop!

Sarita clapped her hands and hugged Anita Aunty.

Gently taking the cat into her hands she said, "Thank you, aunty! I can't believe this! I wanted to bring this very cat home. But I couldn't, as my pocket money didn't suffice." "Thank your Dad, sweetheart," said Anita aunty. "I **bumped** into him in front of the shopping ARCADE. I was looking for a gift for you. He suggested that I buy you this fluffy milky white cat."

"**FANTASTIC**!" Sarita exclaimed, "I'll name it Tubby."

What's in Sarita's Hair?

Sarita was touched by her Dad's THOUGHTFULNESS. She called her best friend Rupa over for lunch and told her about the wonderful **Coincidences**.

Rupa was amazed.

She stroked Sarita's hair and said, "Wait! I think there is an **INSECT** in your hair." She pulled out a thick black **pen-drive**-like object with a black tail, "Is it a new kind of hair clip?"

Sarita placed it on her **DRESSING TABLE**. "That's not my clip. I don't know where it came from and how it got stuck to my hair. I must show it to Ma and Dad."

The Missing 'Pen-drive'

After Rupa left, Sarita called Ma to her room to show the funny-looking object that had come out of her hair. She had kept it on her dressing table, but it was gone!

Tubby sat on Sarita's bed, satisfied after her meal.

When Sarita's Dad, who was a scientist, returned home from his research **laboratory**, he was in for a shock.

"Sarita, since when did you start eating rats?" He asked.

"Rats?" Sarita was stunned, "Dad I was just going to thank you for the pizzas and tell Aunty about my wish to get this cat."

Dad scratched his head in **confusion.** He stroked Sarita's hair and said, "Hey! Did you remove the black clip-like object with a tail from your hair?" he asked anxiously. "Yes, my friend Rupa did it for me," said Sarita, "I wonder what that was." "Oh no!" Dad slapped his forehead, "That was the thought-**TRACKING** device I had attached to your

head. That's how I read your mind - your desire to eat pizzas and to buy this cat from the pet shop."

"The what?" said Sarita.

Dad's Invention gets 'Eaten'

Dad reached into his pocket and fished out a small transmitter. "That black pen-drive-like object relays your thoughts to this device. This is my latest invention after a **DECADE** of **INTENSIVE** research. I have to fasten the thought machine to your hair again. Where is it?!"

"It was right here, on the dressing table. I have no idea where it could have gone. Rats!" Sarita frowned. "Rats..rats..rats!" said Dad, "You are only thinking of juicy and plump rats!"

"No I'm not, Dad!" **SHRIEKED** Sarita. "Ah, I see!" Dad made a startling discovery, "It's your dear cat who has gobbled up the device. I have been reading her thoughts all this while."

"Can't blame poor Tubby," said Sarita, picking up her fluffy cat and stroking her fur, "The device looked like a rat anyway."

Dad's Memory-loss

"I think your cat needs an **operation** to take hat thought-tracking device out of its tummy," Dad tickled Tubby's **UNDERBELLY**. Suddenly, Tubby started clearing his throat. Cats usually cough up furballs, but Tubby coughed something else up. It shot out of his mouth and hit Dad right between his eyes.

"Ooouchh!" howled Dad. It was the thought machine, and it had struck him on his forehead, between his eyebrows. The

IMPACT of the blow made Dad forgets all about his breakthrough invention. Sarita tried to revive Dad's memories of how he had invented the thought-gadget, and Tubby purred and hopped onto his lap; but Dad simply could not track down anyone's thoughts ever again, not even Sarita's.

"Don't worry," laughed Ma when she heard the story of Dad's thought machine and how it FIZZLED out, "To us, he'll always be our very own Einstein!"

TIME TRAVEL

Sahir learnt about time zones in school. He is curious about what time it is in his favourite tourist destinations. On the basis of time difference, find out what time it is in each city and write it in the table below.

Clues:
1. It is 7:30 pm in Mumbai, India.
2. London is behind India by 4 hours and 30 minutes.
3. Rome is behind India by 3 hours and 30 minutes.
4. New York is behind India by 9 hours and 30 minutes.
5. Tokyo is ahead of India by 3 hours and 30 minutes.

Monument	City	Time
	London	
	Rome	
	New York	
	Tokyo	

Sir Humphry Davy
By Pankaj Roy

Penzance, England, was a 17th-century village situated near the sea. It was a small village covered with dense forests. There were mountains, valleys and mines at some distance from the village. The villagers worked in the mines for a living.

Humphry Davy was a resident of this village. He was a thoughtful child. Sitting near the seashore, he would stare at the waves, lost in deep thoughts. He had good analytical skills, an eye for detail and a wild IMAGINATION.

While Humphry's friends were playing and having fun, he studied the mountains. Sometimes, he tasted the SEAWATER and wondered why it was salty. "What in the sea water gives it a salty taste?" he thought.

A Lamp that does not give Light

Young Humphry was more keen on studying nature than school books. He studied trees, birds, animals, wildlife, sky, mountains and stones and made notes in his diary. One day, Humphry drew a picture of a strange lamp in his notebook. It was an oil lamp covered by a mesh of olive branches. "How foolish is this!" laughed his friend, looking at the picture, "If you make a web of **OLIVE** branches over the lamp, they will burn up."

"And the web will decrease the brightness of light. What is the use of designing a lamp that doesn't provide enough light?" added another. "Now, please stop drawing such useless pictures and come out to play with us," they insisted.

Humphry replied, "I am sorry, I won't be able to join you. I have borrowed a book on **Chemistry** from the library, which I plan to read all day." While reading the book, he also conducted some of the experiments mentioned in it. He did not have enough resources, and managed with whatever little he had. He used his kitchen stove as a laboratory burner to conduct heat-based experiments. He got so *engrossed* with his work that he often forgot to eat. Sometimes, he stayed up all night, conducting experiments.

From 'Laughing Stock' to 'Laughing Gas'

When he grew up, Humphry developed a keen interest in Gases. He made a gas that would make one laugh uncontrollably upon sniffing it. Scientists believed that the gas was poisonous and could be fatal to human beings and animals. But Humphry was sure it was not. He inhaled the gas several times himself, and proved it was not fatal. He insisted that the gas could be used for beneficial purposes. The chemical name of that gas is **NITROUS OXIDE** - also known as 'Laughing Gas'. It became known to reduce the sensation of pain. Medical practitioners, especially dentists, soon accepted Humphry Davy's research and started making their patients inhale laughing gas before surgeries. Humphry Davy became famous all over owing to this finding.

Humphry Davy then started research on electricity. He discovered that if light was passed through water, it split into hydrogen and oxygen molecules. This was known as **ELECTROLYSIS**. He passed light through various acids, solutions and mixtures and noticed the chemical changes that took place in the mixtures. Humphry also extracted salt from the sea and studied it. He discovered two elements called **sodium** and *potassium* in it. Sodium is a very active salt. It caught fire when it came in contact with water and had to be stored, immersed in oil. The discovery of sodium and potassium was another feather in Humphry Davy's cap.

Davy's Lamp Saves the Day

During those times, people frequently faced **explosions** in mines. The primary reason for the explosions was **COMBUSTIBLE** gases called **FIREDAMP**, usually made up of **METHANE** that accumulated in large amounts in the coal mines. People had to light lamps to see in the dark mines. Lighting lamps in the presence of damp gases caused mine explosions and many people lost their lives. Sir Humphry Davy started studying combustible gases in 1815. He found that damp gases required a lot of air and high temperatures to catch fire. He also found that these gases did not catch fire when placed in a metal container, as the metal reduced the surrounding temperature. Humphry Davy invented the first safety lamp based on this principle. He made a thick elemental mesh around the light. The light shone bright inside the mesh lamp in the mines. The metal framework lowered the temperature, eliminating the risk of an explosion. This discovery was considered no less than a **MIRACLE**. The lamp allowed miners to work safely. This lamp was named 'Davy's Safety Lamp'.

Little Humpry becomes Sir Davy

The lamp looked a lot like Humphry Davy had drawn in his childhood. The only difference was that this lamp had a metal framework instead of the olive twigs in the drawing. Due to his discoveries and inventions, he was knighted as Sir Humphry Davy and proved that imagination can be a gateway to reality.

A Papery Journey
By Parul Maheshwari

Piku was missing her Grandma. The last time she'd seen her, was during the summer holidays. She asked her parents many times to take her to her Grandma's place, but going there meant taking leave and missing out on classes.

The half-yearly exams at Piku's school had just gotten over and it was announced that the students would get a 4-day holiday. Piku knew just where she wanted to spend them.

That evening, Piku told her father, "Dad, the next four days are holidays. I want to go to Grandma's house!"

Piku and the Magazine

Piku's father agreed and the family started packing. The next morning, half-an-hour before their train was due to arrive, Piku, her sister Pranshu and their parents were at the station. There were many stalls at the platform. Piku saw a magazine stall and her eyes grew wide. She asked her father to buy her a magazine.

"Which magazine do you want, Piku?" her father asked.

Piku looked at all the magazines and pointed at a colourful one. Her father bought it for her.

"You can read this once we're on the train," he said.

Soon enough, their train arrived, and they boarded it together. Piku settled down in a window seat and pulled out her magazine. The magazine's cover had a picture of a hippo with birds sitting on its back. She showed it to her sister, "Look, this is so funny!"

After gazing at the cover for some time, Piku opened the magazine. As she was reading it, Piku couldn't help but feel admiration for the person who invented **paper.** "If it weren't for paper, I would've never been able to read this wonderful magazine," she mused, and said aloud to her father, "Dad, I wonder who invented paper."

The Story of Paper

Piku's father smiled, "Paper was invented in ancient China between the year 220 and 206 BC, Piku dear. From there, it made its way to India through the 'Silk Route'. Europe and Africa got paper much later."

Piku's father further explained, "Did you know that paper, as we know it, was initially used as a packing material and that actual writing was done on calfskin and palm leaves?"

"Today, paper can be made from grass, bamboo, banana stem fiber and even elephant-poo! But most of our paper comes from trees. You do know that trees are important, which is why we should not waste any paper," explained Piku's father. Piku listened intently.

Piku's father then asked, "There is one more invention that plays an important role in ensuring that you get your favourite magazines and books regularly."

"Which is that invention, Dad?"

A Pressing Matter

"Why, the printing press, of course!" Piku's father replied as he kept a lookout for the station they had to get off at. "Wooden **stamps** which have letters carved into them are ARRANGED on a moveable plate and paper is passed beneath. The wooden stamps make an impression on the

paper, and that's how paper gets printed." Piku asked, "Who invented the printing press, Dad?"

"It was invented in Germany by Johannes Gutenberg in the year 1439. But with the introduction of offset printing, the printing press was phased out. The magazine you are reading was surely printed at an offset press," Piku's father pointed out.

"With this, it became easier to spread knowledge and share ideas, and more people got into the habit of reading and writing."

As Piku and her father chatted away, the train pulled into their destination - Grandma's village. It was time to get off and Piku placed the magazine **CAREFULLY** in her bag.

When they reached Grandma's house, Piku's excitement knew no bounds. She was grinning ear-to-ear as she leapt into her Grandma's arms. The next four days were going to be so much fun! "I must ask Dad to buy me a notebook," she thought as she sat on her Grandma's lap and played, "I really want to write everything I've learnt about paper, on paper!"

News Match

Match these five world-famous scientists to their headlines.

James Watt

Charles Darwin

Galileo Galilei

Isaac Newton

Ada Lovelace

The News — Man Evolved From the Apes!

The News — Gravity Discovered!

The News — First Computer Algorithm Written!

The News — Earth Is Not Flat But Round!

The News — Steam Engine Invented!

Slurpy the Survivor
By Kumud Kumar

A black dog with brown patches settled down to live in the yard of the Housing Society where Neelu resided with her parents and Grandma. The residents named her 'Kaali' because of her colour. She was a stray, but everyone treated her with a lot of love and compassion.

One fine day, Kaali gave birth to six tiny puppies and began nursing them in an old deserted room on the society's premises.

Two of the puppies died within a few days because of the cold weather. The remaining four followed Kaali wherever she went.

One of the four puppies grew weaker as days went by, while the others actively raced around Kaali. The weak one fell behind, and began wandering around all by itself.

Neelu **ADORED** dogs and felt sorry for the puppy.

One day, she caught him **moping** and **WHINING**

all by himself and couldn't bear it anymore. She picked him up and carried him into her house. There, she placed a small bowl of milk and biscuits on the floor. The puppy slurped up the milk in a **JIFFY**, and Neelu decided to name him 'Slurpy'. After the treat, Neelu gently picked Slurpy up, and left him outside.

Neelu beats the Theory of Evolution

It became a **routine**. Whenever Neelu found Slurpy wandering alone, she brought him home and gave him a small meal.

Neelu also played with Slurpy, who seemed to enjoy her company.

By that time, the other three puppies lost their lives in road accidents. One was hit by a truck, another one came under the wheels of a car, and the third one fell into a drain.

On the other hand, Slurpy gained strength and became healthier under Neelu's care.

Watching him getting stronger, Neelu's grandmother complimented her, "Neelu, you have proven Charles Darwin's theory wrong by taking care of Slurpy and helping him survive!"

"How is that, Grandma?" Neelu asked, wide-eyed.

"According to Darwin, nature has a mechanism that selects those who are fit to survive. The ones who are weak and unhealthy, tend to die. It is nature's way of **eliminating** those who are not fit to survive. But you have completely **disproved** the theory by caring for Slurpy and

making him a survivor!" "Grandma, I had no idea about Darwin or his theory when I took care of Slurpy. I simply felt bad for him as he was so weak," Neelu replied. "Neelu, compassion is the greatest quality in any human being. We can protect the weak from being BULLIED by the strong. This is what differentiates **civil society** from the jungle," Grandma explained, "The probability of Slurpy dying was the greatest, since he was the weakest, but you changed that."

Neelu was curious, now that she was understanding what her Grandma was saying. She asked, "Grandma, please tell me who Darwin was?"

The Revolutionary Theory of Evolution

"Charles Darwin was a **revolutionary** scientist. He was born on February 12, 1809, in England," said Grandma.

"Why was Darwin revolutionary, Grandma?" Neelu **QUERIED.**

"Darwin was revolutionary as he introduced a completely breakthrough theory called 'The Theory of Evolution'. His ideas challenged the beliefs and notions of many at that time," explained Grandma.

"What were these new ideas?

"In his book, 'The Origin of Species', published on

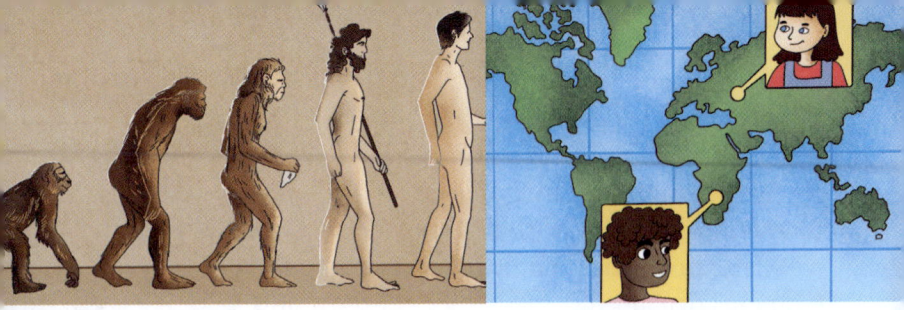

November 24, 1859, Darwin introduced **unique** theories that created a huge **controversy** in Europe and angered many experts," said Grandma.

Neelu **FROWNED**.

Grandma smiled and replied, "He said that the existence of hundreds of species of living beings on earth was a result of evolution, not a gift from God. Until then, it was believed that everything on this earth was created by God."

"Oh, but Grandma, we are still taught that everything is God's creation. So is that untrue?" Neelu asked with surprise.

"It is not like that, Neelu. Changes are always taking place in nature. According to Darwin's 'Theory of Evolution', new species are being created constantly in the animal and the plant kingdoms, but this process is very slow. It takes a million years for any new species to **DEVELOP**. God probably has no role to play in it," Grandma explained. Neelu was amazed by what she heard and said, "Grandma, what you are telling me is very important. Can you explain that to me with some examples, please?" "The climate and geography of a region have a huge impact on the evolution of its **FLORA AND FAUNA.** As you must have noticed, people living in colder regions are generally fair-skinned and those living in warmer regions are dark-skinned. Even people living in the northern parts of our country are fairer than those living in its southern parts. That is the result of different climatic conditions," Grandma explained.

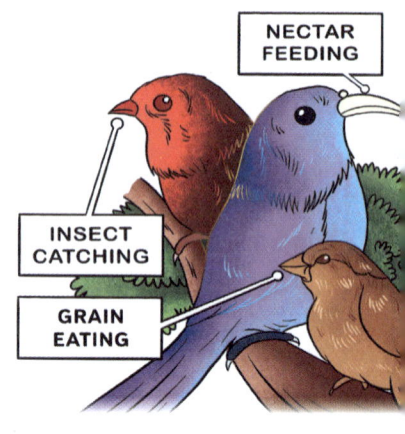

"Wow, Grandma! That is an excellent example. I could never understand why people in Africa are dark-skinned and those living in Europe are fair-skinned. Now I know!" said Neelu, excitedly.

A Scientific Approach

Excited by Neelu's interest in the subject, Grandma **quizzed** her, "Neelu, tell me how many different kinds of **BEAKS** you have noticed in birds?".

"What kind of a question is that, Grandma? There must be at least a hundred different kinds of beaks that can be found among birds. Some birds have strong beaks, some small, some long, some even have hook-like beaks!" Neelu laughed.

"And do you know why that is? Darwin has explained this. Birds that feed on grains have thicker beaks, the ones that suck nectar from flowers have sharp, thin beaks, and birds that prey on fish have long, strong beaks. Their beaks have changed and evolved, based on what they eat," Grandma explained. "Wow, Grandma! The earth is so **DIVERSE**. The birds and animals that live here have changed over time to suit their surroundings and lifestyles!" Neelu **AFFIRMED**. Grandma was happy that Neelu was able to understand the science of evolution at such a young age. She continued, "Neelu, this is called a scientific approach, and the sooner the world starts to think scientifically, the better it is for all of us!"

"Grandma, I want to learn more about Darwin and his theories. I am going to read the book and try to understand why birds and animals behave the way they do," said Neelu. "Yes, Neelu. All children should understand the importance of science and develop a curiosity for it, just like you have!" Grandma smiled.

"I want to be well-informed, Grandma," said Neelu, a rather serious expression on her face.

All of a sudden, they heard someone whimpering by the door. It was Slurpy! "Slurpy is hungry. EXCUSE me, Grandma, I have to feed him," Neelu DEFTLY picked up Slurpy as he came bounding towards her.

"I'm going to give you extra milk today," she whispered, as she carried him to the kitchen. Slurpy deserved the reward. After all, it was because of him that Neelu had learnt the 'Theory of Evolution' that day.

The Burj Ice-scraper
By Rohini Chintha

Anu looked unhappily at her ice-cream. "Grandpa, I want a bigger one, with a hundred scoops on it!" she demanded.

"A bigger one?" said Grandpa, surprised. "You already have three scoops of ice-cream stacked one on top of the other on the cone, Anu. If you add any more **scoops**, they will topple!" he said, trying to reason with her.

Anu turned a **deaf** ear to Grandpa's logic. "I want many more scoops. A hundred more, at least," she frowned.

"You can eat as much ice-cream as you want, but have one scoop at a time; not all at the same time. Even if they don't **TOPPLE**, by the time you get through a couple of scoops the rest melt." explained Grandpa.

Anu **WAILED**, " I want a hundred scoops on my ice-cream cone, Grandpa. Even if you say they would topple and melt, I still want it!" Anu was **adamant**. The ice-cream scoops on her cone were beginning to melt, and instead of eating them, she was crying for more.

The Ice-cream Skyscraper

Grandpa lifted Anu in his arms and asked her gently, "Why do you want a hundred scoops on your ice-cream, Anu?" "Well," said Anu wiping her tears, "I want to have the tallest ice-cream in the whole world."

"Where did you get the idea from?" asked Grandpa, surprised.

"I came up with it myself," Anu sniffled, "I want to have the tallest ice-cream in the whole world, and I am going to call it my skyscraper ice-cream," she replied.
"Skyscraper ice-cream!" Grandpa repeated, "Wonderful idea! Why a hundred scoops though? Even 10 scoops could make it the tallest ice-cream," he suggested.

"That's not possible," Anu **pouted**, "For a building to be called a skyscraper, it should have at least 40 floors. A building with even 39 floors will not qualify."

Grandpa was pleasantly surprised. He wanted to know what else was on Anu's mind. "Well in that case, 40 scoops of ice-cream stacked on top of each other should do. Why a 100?"

"Oh Grandpa!" Anu was annoyed, "Forty is the minimum number. That doesn't make it the tallest in the whole world. I want my skyscraper ice-cream to match the world's tallest skyscraper - the Burj Khalifa in Dubai! Hence, I need at least a hundred scoops." Before Grandpa could answer, another idea struck Anu. "Grandpa! If I can have 200 scoops, it will be taller than Burj Khalifa, which has only 154 floors."

Grandpa nodded, amused. Anu continued excitedly, "You know what we will call our ice-cream then, Grandpa? We will call it - Anu & Grandpa's Burj Ice-Scraper!"

Skyscrapers of all Sorts

While Anu talked, Grandpa noticed that the ice-cream they had bought was melting. The cone had become soft too. "Well, dear ice-cream-ARCHITECT," said Grandpa, putting her down, "There is just one problem with the idea."

Anu looked up inquiringly. Grandpa pointed to the melting ice-cream and Anu started licking it hungrily. "The scoops at the bottom might melt by the time the 100th scoop is placed," he said.

"We could build our skyscraper with a different material...," Anu trailed off, "How about a muffin skyscraper?"

"How will you stick them one on top of the other?" Grandpa asked her. "With **whipped cream**, of course!" said Anu. "Fair enough," said Grandpa thoughtfully, "But wouldn't CONSTRUCTION blocks be better-suited to building a skyscraper?" he asked.

"No!" PROTESTED Anu, "I can't eat them, can I?". "How about clay?" Grandpa persisted, "Why do you want to make a skyscraper with food material and then eat it all up? Don't you want to show it to your friends?"

Anu agreed and decided to get on board with Grandpa's idea. Anu and her Grandpa went home and began building the tallest tower they possibly could, with **modelling clay**. Anu's friends, who came over to play with her, joined in.

Finally when it was done, the clay skyscraper looked truly **GRAND**. Everyone loved it! A few weeks later, on Anu's birthday, Grandpa surprised her with a skyscraper cake, which had 'Anu's Burj Cake-Scraper' written on it in **ICING**. Anu loved the surprise. She was happy that her idea to make skyscrapers out of any possible material, was being appreciated. The cake was delicious and everyone relished it, down to the last **crumb.**

The Gift of Braille

By Laxmi Kanodia

Tanmay was walking to the market with his grandfather when he noticed a blind man STRUGGLING to cross the busy road. Just then, a boy rushed over to help the man safely reach the other side.

Curious, Tanmay asked, "Dadaji, if blind people have trouble crossing the road, how do they read or manage their daily activities? It must be so hard for them!"

"You're right, Tanmay. We'll talk more about this when we get home," his grandfather replied.

Later, at home, as Dadaji sipped his coffee, he began to explain. "Eyes are one of nature's most PRECIOUS gifts to us. But some people are either born without sight or lose it later in life. Though they face challenges, science has made it possible for them to live independently, just like anyone else. One of the most important tools they have is the Braille script, which allows them to read and receive an education."

"That's amazing! Who invented Braille, Dadaji? Was it a blind person?" Tanmay asked eagerly.

The Story of Louis Braille

"Well," Dadaji began, "Louis Braille, the inventor of the Braille script, wasn't born blind. He lost his sight in an **accident** when he was a young boy. While studying, he realised that the existing methods for blind people to read were INADEQUATE. Louis was passionate about learning and wanted to help others like him read with ease."

Tanmay leaned in, **INTRIGUED**. "Tell me more about Louis Braille, Dadaji."

"Louis was born on January 4, 1809, in a small village called Coupvray in France. He was the youngest of four children. His father, Simon Lele Braille, worked as a SADDLER for the royal horses, and Louis often played in his father's

workshop. One day, when Louis was just three, he injured his eye while playing. His mother quickly bandaged it, thinking it was a minor injury."

"What happened next?" Tanmay asked, his hands cupping his face.

"At first, the family thought Louis would recover. But he developed an **INFECTION**, which worsened and spread to his other eye. By the age of eight, Louis was completely blind," Dadaji continued.

"Despite losing his sight, Louis would walk with a cane to visit the local **priest** and listen to stories. He even attended the town school. But one day, when the other children were reading a poem, Louis felt tears in his eyes because he couldn't join them."

Just then, Tanmay's friends called him to come outside and play, but Tanmay was too **ABSORBED** in the story. "I'm not coming today!" he shouted, turning back to Dadaji. "Please continue."

The Need for a New Script

Dadaji smiled and went on, "With the help of the priest, Louis was admitted to the Royal Institute for Blind Children. There, he learned **weaving** and **leatherwork**, but his love for reading never **FADED**. The school used a **script** for the visually impaired, created by Valentine Haüy, but it wasn't easy to use. Louis knew something better was needed."

"So, what did he do?" Tanmay asked eagerly.

"He invented a new system!" Dadaji replied. "While at the school, Louis met a French army **officer** named Captain Charles Barbier. The captain had developed a system called **SONOGRAPHY,** which soldiers used to read in the dark. It involved raised letters on paper, and this inspired Louis. Using the idea, he created a script with six raised dots, which was easier to read and allowed for 64 different letters and symbols. This system became known as Braille. Louis introduced it in 1824, when he was just 15 years old, and it was officially published in 1829."

A Gift to the World

"Wow! He was so young!" Tanmay exclaimed, clapping his hands. "But Dadaji, what about other subjects like math and music?" "Good question!" Dadaji said with affection. "Louis didn't stop at just letters. He later developed symbols for mathematics and music. Thanks to Braille, education for **VISUALLY IMPAIRED** people improved dramatically, and today, the system is recognized and used all over the world."

"Wow Dadaji," Tanmay exclaimed. "I hope one day science will **ADVANCE** enough to help blind people regain their sight."

"If more children made wishes like you, that day might come sooner than we think," Dadaji said with a smile. "Now go play with your friends!"

BRAILLE DECODE

PUZZLE TIME

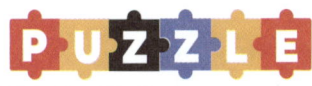

Yash's mother has left an encouraging note in braille for him. Find out what the note says by using the guide given below.

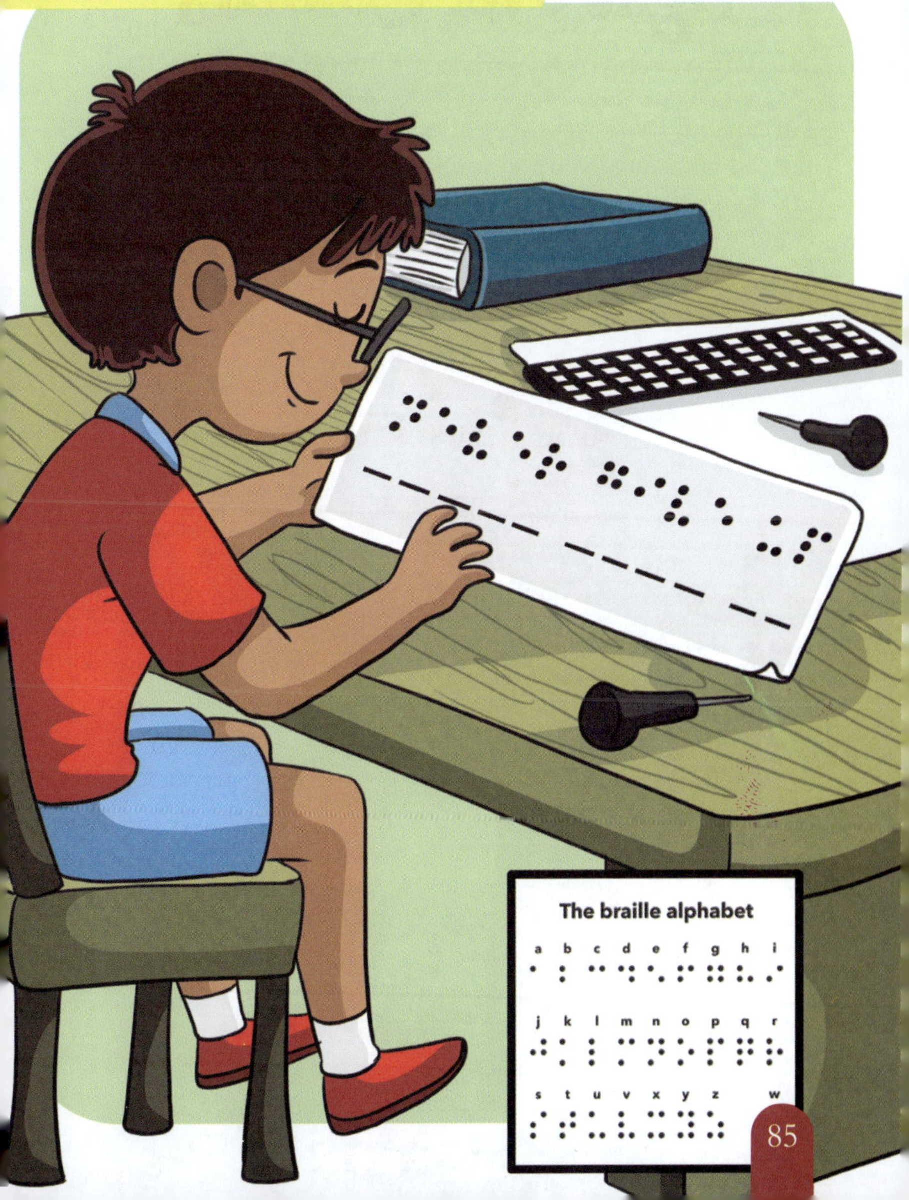

A Fight over Colours
By Vijay Ghanshyamdas Khatri

Farhan and Raisa were very affectionate towards each other but did occasionally argue and fight, like any other brother and sister. Colourful things like school bags, balloons could start a fight between them, and so could games like **Carrom** or **Ludo**.

That day they were fighting again and it was over a red rose. It had **BLOOMED** in their garden, and both Farhan and Raisa wanted it. Farhan managed to pluck it for himself. Raisa complained to their father, "Papa, Farhan fights with me every day. Yesterday he wouldn't give me the yellow balloon and today he ran away with my favourite flower, the red rose!" Papa laughed, "If I said that a red rose is not red and a yellow balloon is not yellow, would you still fight over them?"

"To end our fight, you have resorted to science again, Papa!" Farhan walked in with the red rose. "It's all yours, Raisa," he gave the flower to his sister. "Papa will now tell us something interesting about it." Raisa took the rose from Farhan. **Admiring** the deep red colour of each petal she asked their father, "What are you saying, Papa? I can only see the colour 'red' in this rose!"

The Glass Prism Demonstration

Papa took something out of the cupboard. It was a **glass prism**. He placed it on the table near a window, and positioned it carefully so that sunlight went right through it. He then positioned a sheet of white paper on the other side of the prism. A rainbow-like **spectrum** of seven colours **projected** themselves onto the paper! Both Farhan and Raisa **gasped** in wonder.

Their father said, "Did you know that light is made up of seven different colours? Violet, indigo, blue, green, yellow, orange and red."

Raisa clapped, "This is fascinating Papa! But what does it have to do with the red rose?"

"When rays of light fall on a rose, all the other colours except for red are **absorbed** by the rose. It reflects red alone which is why it appears red," Papa told them.

Farhan considered this for a moment and asked, "Does this mean no object has its own colour? And it appears to be the colour it **REFLECTS**?"

Raisa piped in, "What happens if an object absorbs all of the colours that exist, and reflects none? What does it look like then?" "An object that absorbs all the colours and reflects none, appears black," their father replied. Farhan asked,

"And what if an object reflects all of the colours and absorbs none?" "Excellent question, Farhan. That object will appear white. Do you understand now?" Farhan and Raisa nodded.

The 'Colour' Scientists

Their father smiled and said, "Now look upwards and tell me – what is the colour of the sky?" "It looks blue," said Raisa, "But the sky is not an object, is it? How is light absorbed or reflected by it?"

Their father explained, "The earth is surrounded by the atmosphere which is made up of **particles**.

RENOWNED scientist Lord Walter Rayleigh said that when light passes through particles of air in the sky, the particles act like objects and absorb or reflect it. During that process, the colour blue is reflected more than any other colour, which is why the sky appears blue to us. Also, our eyes have special cells called '**RODS**' and '**cones**' which are very sensitive and perceive colour."

Farhan pressed on, "How about spaces that are much higher up

in the sky, where there is no atmosphere? What colour is that?"

"That would be Space to us, and it appears black. Astronauts who travel deep into space, **PERCEIVE** a 'black' sky."
"Papa, what colour is the ocean? I think it is blue." Raisa said.

Their father countered, "Why do you say so?"

"Papa, the sky is blue, and its reflection falls on the ocean. So the ocean appears blue. Isn't that right?"

Their father replied, "We should credit Dr. C.V. Raman for the answer to this question."

"Who was he, Papa?"" Farhan and Raisa asked in one voice.
"He was a great Indian scientist, my children," their father replied, "He was born on November 7, 1888, and had a keen interest in scientific research. Dr. Raman left a high-paying job in Kolkata to work as a professor at a university. He conducted many experiments using **CRYSTALS, MAGNETS, X-RAYS**, and light. In 1921, he attended a conference conducted by Oxford University, England. Afterwards while returning on a ship, he observed that the ocean appeared blue throughout, and did research as to why that was so." Farhan and Raisa were listening, rapt.

"At that time, even Lord Rayleigh had said that the ocean appears blue because it reflects the blue sky. But Dr. Raman was not satisfied with the theory. Using a **SPECTROMETER** on the ship's deck, he found out that the ocean was blue from top to bottom. Not only that, it appears blue even when the sky is clouded over;" their father told them, "That means that the ocean's blue colour is because of the water itself."

Farhan exclaimed, "That means that the ocean is not blue because it reflects the sky above." "Absolutely!" Their father was happy that his children were understanding the **concept** of colours,

"When Dr. Raman returned to India, he argued that water molecules, like air particles in the sky, reflect the colour blue of the sun's rays, and that's why the ocean appears blue." "This is **fascinating**!" Raisa said excitedly.

Roses and Balloons!

Their father continued, "Yes it is! Once, Dr. Raman and his colleagues were studying the **SCATTERING** of light. They were trying to pass rays of light through a **BEAKER** containing a liquid called '**benzene**', using a spectrometer.

They found that there were several lines of other colours around the main line of light. That meant, they were seeing lines of mixed colours, radiating from the central line of light.

"Why did that happen, Papa?" asked Farhan.

"Light appeared to behave like solid particles, which was a big surprise to them," their father replied, "Upon further research, Dr. Raman and his team observed that when light passes through a solid, liquid, or gaseous medium, its rays collide with particles in the medium. Part of the light gets scattered in other directions, like a cricket ball **colliding** with a football, **BOUNDING** off it, and

moving in another direction." Papa paused, and continued, "This means the energy of light particles can change.

Dr. Raman devoted himself completely to this discovery, which till today is called **The Raman Effect**."
"Wow, Papa!" Farhan and Raisa were amazed.

"Dr. Raman made this discovery on February 28, 1928. He was awarded the Nobel Prize in 1930 for his contribution to the world of science, and was the first Asian to receive this honour." Papa explained with a smile.

Raisa inhaled the **FRAGRANCE** of the red rose, lifted it into the light and said, "Dr. Raman's research and **DISCOVERIES** have opened many doors, Papa. I feel like the whole world has been coloured by him, including my red rose!"

Farhan said, "To see something ordinary from a different **angle** can lead to a great **discovery**. That's what Dr. C.V. Raman has taught us."

"And you both were fighting over roses and balloons!" Papa joked. Farhan and Raisa looked at each other and laughed, "Don't worry Papa, we'll soon find something better to fight about!"

Who made the Model?

By Vandana Gupta

As soon as their science teacher Miss Sonali entered Class VI, the children went quiet.

"Children, I hope you remember that your exams will start soon," she said **STERNLY**.

"Each one of you has to complete a project," she continued, "You may choose from any topic that you have studied so far, or will study soon, and make a model in **CONTEXT** to it. You have 10 days to complete and present your models."

The students immediately started discussing what **mOdE** to make.

"Remember, children, the marks you score in the **PROJECT** will be added to your half-yearly **GRADE**!", Miss Sonali informed them.

At the end of the ten-day mark, Miss Sonali announced, "All of you should bring your models tomorrow and keep them in the Science Lab. During the science period, I will give each one of you two minutes to **PRESENT** your model."

The next day, as soon as the children reached school, they kept their models in the Science Lab. When they returned from the assembly, Vihaan was already seated in the class.

"You didn't attend the assembly today, Vihaan?" Amit asked.

"I was late, so I came straight to the class," Vihaan replied.

The Childrens' Wonderful Models

Soon enough, the bell for their science period rang, and everyone walked to the lab. Miss Sonali was already there, waiting for them. The children were excited and stood next to their models, eager to present them. "You all have worked hard and made wonderful models!" said Ms. Sonali, "I now invite you to come up here one by one and present them."

Sonam who was fond of music, had made the model of a **'Jal Tarang'**, a musical **INSTRUMENT**. She filled bowls with water at different levels, and tapped across them with a pair of sticks to create varied musical notes. She played the tune of the song 'We Shall Overcome' on her model.

"Tell us something about it. How are the different notes produced?" Miss Sonali asked. "Miss, this is a very old Indian instrument. Earlier, it used to be played with metal bowls. When musicians experimented with china-clay bowls for the same, they realised that the sound produced

was sweeter. When sound waves travel through water, the difference in the water-level in each bowl produces a different musical note. The lower the water level, the higher the NOTE. When the water level is increased, the note becomes lower. If we understand this and PRACTICE, we can play any tune!" Sonam explained.

It was Nakul's turn next. He had placed two flowers—one with a blue TINT and one pure white—with their stalks intact, in two different glasses. One glass had normal water and the other had water with INK added to it.

"Nakul, what have you made?" Miss Sonali asked.

"Miss, I **EXPERIMENTED** to see how the **stalks** of a plant transport water and other natural resources to all its parts, up to the flower. The flower which is in the glass filled with ink-water, has become blue, whereas the flower in the normal water has remained white." Nakul explained.

"Very interesting!" said Miss Sonali.

"Miss, I had made a model on gears, but Vihaan is standing near it and claiming it is his model!" Aarav complained loudly before Miss Sonali could choose the next student.

"Aarav, you can speak when it is your turn," said Miss Sonali.

"But, Miss! Vihaan's name is written on it! I think he wrote it himself. " Aarav sounded QUITE worried.

"Aarav, tell me about it when it's your turn.", Miss Sonali said firmly, and Aarav had to remain quiet.

Monika had made a water filter. She had cut the bottom of a PLASTIC bottle and covered its mouth with a cotton cloth. She had placed it upside down in a plastic container, and had arranged a layer of sand over it, followed by a layer of **charcoal** pieces. She had topped it with **GRAVEL.**

Monika demonstrated her model by pouring dirty water from the top, and the entire class watched as clean water collected drop-by-drop into the container at the bottom.

Amit had made a **BATTERY** by **embedding** two nails into a potato. One nail was made of **zinc**, and the other was made of **copper**. He connected a wire to both the nails and powered a small electrical bulb with this contraption. The bulb lit up, much to the delight of the class and Miss Sonali.

"Similarly, we can turn ORANGES and LEMONS into batteries!" Amit told the class, "Electricity is produced when electrons travel through two metals in an ACIDIC medium,"

"Well done!" said Miss Sonali and moved to the next table where Vihaan and Aarav stood together.

Resolving the Fight

Vihaan's name was written on the model, whereas Aarav was insisting that he had made it. It was time for Miss Sonali to address this **COMPLICATED** situation. "Alright, tell me how you made this model, and what does it show?" Miss Sonali asked Aarav.

"I cut out four discs of different sizes from cardboard, Miss," Aarav was relieved to be able to explain, "I made wooden **spikes** of equal length and pinned them at the centre of the cardboard discs in such a way that they could be rotated. I arranged the four discs touching each other, so that when one disc is **rotated**, the second, third and fourth discs also rotate simultaneously."

"While the discs are rotating, we can see that in the time taken by the largest disc to complete one rotation, the smaller discs can complete three to four rotations," he continued.

"If there are 40 spikes on the largest disc and 10 spikes on the smaller disc, when the largest disc rotates only once, the smaller discs rotate three to four times in the same given time. The speed of the smaller discs is higher than that of the larger ones.

Gears of cars work similarly, based on the same science and they help the car to move at different speeds on different gears.

To make the model **ATTRACTIVE**, I painted each part a different colour." Aarav concluded.

"Anybody can say this! It is visible on the **model** and Miss Sonali has already taught this in class," Vihaan mocked Aarav. "I will tell you one thing that is not visible," Aarav said, "I painted my model pink and wrote my name in yellow. However, the paint peeled off when I was testing it and therefore I painted over it in brown. When the paint dried, I wrote my name in black," Aarav **DISCLOSED**.

"But I can see that the model is painted blue, with Vihaan's name painted in brown. We'll have to **SCRAPE** off the blue paint to know the truth," Miss Sonali suggested.

Vihaan became agitated. "Miss Sonali, what's the need to do that?"

Vihaan's reaction made Miss Sonali feel that something was **AMISS**. She scratched a little paint off Vihaan's name with the tip of a ruler. There it was! The colours that Vihaan had mentioned, began appearing from underneath the blue paint on more scraping.

Vihaan Presents his Model

"Aarav is right. He has made this model. Vihaan, where is your model? Did you not make one?" Miss Sonali asked.

"No, Ma'am, I did bring in a model," mumbled Vihaan.

"Where is it?"

Vihaan took out a **POTTED** plant from a corner of the lab and placed it on the table. "This is my model."

"What's this?" Miss Sonali asked. "You taught us that when you sow seeds in the soil, they sprout and grow into new plants. I have made a model of that."

"But you have brought a grown-up plant. If you had sown seeds 10 days back, the **seedlings** would be small and wiry, not a big plant like this!" Miss Sonali was not happy, "Okay, Vihaan, when did you repaint and write your name on Aarav's model?"

Vihaan had no choice but to tell the truth. "I went to place my model in the lab and saw the beautiful models made by others. My model looked **POOR** in comparison. So I skipped the assembly and painted my name over Aarav's."

"If only you had used the given 10 days to make a good model, you wouldn't have faced this situation," said Miss Sonali, "I am giving you one week's time to make a new model and submit it, Vihaan. But right now, you must apologise to Aaarav." "I'm sorry, Aarav," Vihaan **extended** his hand. Aarav shook it, glad that he had stood up for himself and his model.

Sequence

February 28 is National Science Day

Scientists follow six steps, referred to as the 'Process of Science', to conduct experiments. Number the boxes in the right sequence.

Experiment

Come to a conclusion

Record data

Think of an idea

Plan your experiment

Research your topic

*Answers on the last page.

Visiting Telephone City

By Ashima Kaushik

Maya's family had recently moved to Toronto, Canada. Everything was new to her—a new city, a new school, new friends, new teachers, a new house, and a new neighbourhood. She was still adjusting but excited by all the changes in her life. So, when Ms. Hardcastle, her teacher, announced a class field trip, Maya couldn't wait.

That afternoon, she eagerly showed her mom the permission form. Her mom signed it without **HESITATION** and noticed there was an option for parents to **VOLUNTEER.** Maya loved the idea of her mom joining them on the trip.

The class was headed to Brantford, a city about two hours away, to visit Bell Homestead, a national **historic** site where Alexander Graham Bell invented the telephone on July 26, 1874.

Mr. Bell's House

On the day of the trip, the students and volunteer parents arrived at school early, gathering around Ms. Hardcastle. She made a final bathroom call and instructed everyone to line up for the bus. Ms. Ruby, the bus driver, blew her whistle and called everyone aboard. Once they were all seated, she quipped, "You can sing and play games, but no asking, 'Are we there yet?'" Everyone giggled.

The journey was lively, and soon they arrived in Brantford, also known as 'Telephone City'. Once they got off the bus, Ms. Hardcastle SPLIT the students into small groups, each with a parent volunteer and a guide from the site.

Mr. Chris, their guide, introduced himself with enthusiasm. "Welcome to the home of Alexander Graham Bell, the inventor of the telephone—an apparatus designed to transmit sound using electrical VIBRATIONS," he announced, his deep voice capturing the group's attention.

Maya and her mom were ENCHANTED by the charming green-and-white house, surrounded by colourful flower bowers and neatly trimmed bushes. Jenny, one of the students, asked in amazement, "Is this really Mr. Bell's house?"

Mr. Chris laughed. "Yes, it is. Today, we'll explore the science behind the telephone. There are fun activities, and we'll see how the Bell family

lived in the 19th century. If you're good, you'll even get to make a call with one of our 1930's TELEPHONES!" "Wow!" the group chorused.

Using a Vintage Telephone

Following Mr. Chris in a neat line, the kids made sure not to touch anything they shouldn't. He explained that although the house had been **restored,** many of the belongings were original **VINTAGE** items. They entered a room filled with telephones of all shapes and sizes, along with scientific INSTRUMENTS and SKETCHES on display.

Maya's mom admired the collection of colourful telephones with their cords, handsets, and dials. Mr. Chris handed the group an old black telephone and asked them to figure out how to use it.

Jenny pressed the numbers, Michael tugged at the cord, and Maya simply picked up the handset, and tapped on it. Mr. Chris and Maya's mom chuckled at their attempts. Mom demonstrated. "You don't press anything, you rotate these numbers here," she said, showing them how to dial.

Mr. Chris added, "That's why we say 'dialling a number.' The part you speak into is the TRANSMITTER, and the other end is the RECEIVER."

Next, they moved to a room showcasing even older telephones with wires, bells, strings, and switches. The group was fascinated by posters depicting the evolution of the telephone from 1875 to 1995.

"The basic design hasn't changed much," Mr. Chris explained, pointing to one of the exhibits. "This is the first telephone, which used a **horseshoe** magnet and other electromagnets. Both the transmitter and receiver worked in a similar way." He paused before continuing, "Do you know how sound travels? It moves through the air as waves, created by something vibrating, like a plucked guitar string or a ringing bell."

"Like the ripples in a pond when you throw a stone?" Maya asked. "Exactly. Those waves move through the air and reach your ears, allowing you to hear sound," he explained. In the next room, an activity table was set up with paper cups, string, paper clips, and thumbtacks.

The Paper-cup Experiment

Mr. Chris instructed everyone to poke a hole in the bottom of two cups and thread a string through each hole, securing it with a paper clip. "These clips will keep the string from dropping out of the cups," he explained. "When you speak into one cup, the sound waves vibrate the cup, which makes the string vibrate. These vibrations travel through the string to the other cup, where they're heard as sound," Mr. Chris said.

Michael asked eagerly, "So, you can hear someone through the other cup?" "Exactly," Mr. Chris replied, stretching the string between two cups. Michael giggled as he listened to Mr. Chris speak into one end. Soon, everyone took turns trying out their **PAPER-CUP** telephones. "Did Alexander Graham Bell really use this idea for the telephone?" the kids asked, wide-eyed.

"Yes, the principle is the same," Mr. Chris confirmed. "The main difference is that the telephone uses electricity instead of a string to transmit sound." "Wow, that's amazing!" Jenny exclaimed.

Just then, Ms. Ruby blew the whistle. Ms. Hardcastle gathered the group for a **headcount** before they boarded the bus. They were off to Lion's Park for a picnic before heading back to Toronto. It had been a **fascinating** day, exploring Telephone City!

The haunted room

By Vivek Chakravarty

"I am so tired! I'm going to have a glass of **LEMONADE** before I get back to work," Jumpy monkey grumbled as he returned home from the market all hot and **SWEATY**.

He opened the door to the room where he kept his **BEVERAGES**, and got the shock of his life. He had left a jug of lemonade on the table, which was now empty. There was not even a drop of it remaining.

"Eh!? Who emptied this **JUG** of lemonade? It certainly wasn't me!"

Jumpy was too tired to think clearly, and decided that perhaps he had already drunk the lemonade and forgotten about it. However, this began to happen every single day and it made him furious.

"It can't be me. There must be some creature around, who drinks my lemonade. Wait till I find out!" Jumpy shouted, shaking his fist in the air.

From that day on, Jumpy started hiding outside the room and kept a watch on the door. Even so, when he opened the room after a while, the lemonade jug on the table would be empty.

Frustrated, Jumpy hired security guards and installed CCTV cameras all around. However, items like lemonade, cold drinks, and water continued to disappear from the room, and there was no trace of the thief.

Jumpy lost his cool and started believing that there was a ghost in the room which was consuming everything Jumpy kept in there. He began avoiding the room entirely, and restricted himself to using the other room in his house.

A Visit from Friends

Days went by until one evening when his old friends Cheeku rabbit and Meeku mouse visited from Champakvan.

Jumpy welcomed them and prepared a delicious meal.

"You've outdone yourself, Jumpy!" Meeku licked his fingers after the feast, "I feel like falling asleep right away. Please show me to my room so I can stretch out on the bed," Meeku said, rubbing his stomach.

"Sorry, Meeku, but you will have to sleep in this room with us," Jumpy said **apologetically.**

"Why Jumpy, is the other room occupied?" Cheeku asked.

"No but…"

"There's an empty room, yet you're asking us to sleep here! Is there any **treasure** in that room?" Meeku teased Jumpy. "You can trust us - we won't even look for it," Cheeku laughed, joining in.

"The other room is quite messy - I haven't cleaned it," Jumpy said, *EMBARRASSED.*

Cheeku was already trying to open the door to the room, "Hey, there are **cobwebs** on this door. It seems like this room hasn't been opened in a while," Cheeku said.

"Yes, that's why it is dirty," Jumpy replied.

"Why don't we check? Between the three of us, I am sure we can clean it up quickly," suggested Meeku.

Jumpy **panicked**, "Wait... don't open the door!"

"What now, Jumpy?" Meeku halted, surprised.

"Cheeku, Meeku! I lied. There's another reason why I never go to that room," Jumpy **CONFESSED**.

"What reason?" Cheeku asked.

Jumpy narrated to them the incidents that were **occurring** in the room, and told them about his conviction that there was a ghost in room.

"Incredible! Someone or something in that room consumes the liquids kept there, but doesn't steal or damage anything else?" Cheeku wondered.

"At first, I even thought maybe someone was playing a joke on me. So, I hired security guards and installed CCTV cameras in the house to identify the culprit, but they didn't help," Jumpy said, taking a deep breath.

"Surely there's some thirsty soul in the room who drinks up all the liquids," Meeku said nervously.

" It can just as easily drink our blood. That's why we shouldn't go into that room," Jumpy warned.

"I'm going inside the room," Cheeku declared, "Both of you stay here." Cheeku opened the latch of the room and went inside. Meeku followed and then a timid Jumpy - all of them sneezing because of the dust. "There's no evidence of anyone living in this room or visiting it frequently," Cheeku said, after inspecting the room. "We'll guard this room starting tomorrow morning and find out what this is all about."

Cheeku becomes a Detective

The next morning, Jumpy filled a jug with water and placed it right in the middle of the table in the haunted room. Cheeku, Meeku and Jumpy guarded the room from outside.

There was no suspicious movement, and by afternoon, their patience ran out. Cheeku decided to open the room and check the jug.

As soon as he reached the table, Cheeku screeched in alarm. The jug was empty!

"Cheeku, see for yourself! We watched the room like hawks but the jug is empty. It can only mean one thing..." Jumpy stammered.

"...that this is a **HAUNTED** room, and there are ghosts here," Meeku completed Jumpy's statement.

"I don't believe it. Tomorrow, I will spend the whole day inside this room and see for myself," Cheeku said.

The next morning, Cheeku placed a jug of water on the table in the room and hid behind a sofa in the 'haunted room'. He kept an eye on the table from his hiding place.

Nobody approached the jug, and the lack of any action made Chekku **DROWSY.** He fell asleep without realising it.

After about an hour, he woke up in utter panic.

"I was supposed to watch the table! Let me check if the jug inside is full or not," Cheeku went to the table and was again greeted by an empty jug.

"Where has the water gone?" Cheeku muttered in surprise and picked up the jug. A loud scream escaped his lips and he placed the jug right back.

"Cheeku, are you okay?" Meeku and Jumpy rushed into the room.

"Yes, everything is fine." "Then why did you scream?" Jumpy asked. "I saw your so-called ghost, and I have also found a way to get rid of it," Cheeku said, smiling.

"What?!" Meeku and Jumpy were taken aback.

"I'll tell you tomorrow," said Cheeku.

The 'Ghost' is Revealed

The next morning, Cheeku hung up **CURTAINS** on every window of the haunted room, blocking out the natural light.

"Cheeku, it has become way too dark in here," Jumpy commented.

"Have some PATIENCE. The ghost of your haunted room is going to be chased out today," Cheeku smiled.

They waited **anxiously**, time passed, and soon it was evening.

"Cheeku, when will the ghost arrive?" Jumpy asked finally, bored out of his wits.

"He has run away."

"Run away? We were right outside and didn't notice anything," Meeku was surprised. "He ran away when we put curtains on the windows and doors of this room. In reality, whatever was happening was science, not ghosts." "Science?"

"Yes. There are many windows in Jumpy's house, especially in this room. SUNLIGHT streams in through all the windows and falls directly on the table in this room. Therefore the jug kept on the table heats up, and the liquid in it EVAPORATES."

"Jumpy, the windows in your house function like a solar cooker! I realisedthis when I tried to pick up the empty jug. It was so hot that it **scalded** my hand," Cheeku explained.

"But whenever I picked up the jug, it was never hot," Jumpy said.

"The jug must have cooled down by that time, Jumpy,". Cheeku offered, and Jumpy nodded.

"It appears that sunlight is the lemonade-thief, but alas, we can't complain about it to the police!" laughed Jumpy. "Well then, let's roll up our sleeves and clean this room, so that we get lots of space to roll around and sleep comfortably tonight!" remarked Meeku, as he went out to fetch the **BROOM** and dustpan.

Sp🛸t the difference

Circle 10 differences you can find between the two pictures.

Us and Them

We stick out our tongues to see how much it can stretch to lick an ice-cream in front of us. Woodpeckers do the same thing when trying to catch insects. It's just that some woodpeckers have tongues that are as long as their bodies!

The average human tongue is 3.9 inches in length, which is a fraction of the length of our body. The Grey-faced Woodpecker has a tongue that is almost 7 inches long, which is about 2.8 times the length of its beak and longer than its entire body. Its barbed tongue acts like a spear to catch insects, when it is stuck into the hollows in tree-trunks.

The woodpecker has a layer of sticky saliva on its tongue to help it catch insects.

But where does it stow away its long tongue? The tongue splits into two and curls back into its head, where it rejoins and inserts itself into its right nostril (as shown in the above illustration).

In spite of having a long tongue, the woodpecker does not have a vocal song. It makes a drumming sound on hollow trees or logs to communicate.

Sahil learns Birdwatching

By Sudha Vijay

One afternoon, Sahil, a class-4 student was returning from school when he heard faint squeaks. He looked around and noticed that they were coming from a tree nearby.

"There are young chicks in that nest. They must be hungry," thought Sahil, looking upwards. Sahil loved birds and wanted to feed the chicks in the nest.

He pulled out the leftover chapatis from his lunchbox and began climbing the tree. When he got closer to the nest, a couple of bigger birds began circling him, chirping noisily. One of them tried to peck at him and Sahil lost his balance. He fell down onto the hard ground.

"Ow!" he cried in pain. Sahil raised his head and saw that

the birds were still hovering over the nest. He quietly picked up his bag and went home.

Uncle Dinesh, the Birdwatcher

Back home, Uncle Dinesh was surprised to see **bruises** on his nephew's arms and knees. "What happened?" he asked with concern. "Nothing, I was doing some BIRD-WATCHING," said Sahil, frowning.

He went on to narrate what had happened. Uncle Dinesh dressed Sahil's wounds, smiled and said, "What you did was the wrong way to approach birds. That's not birdwatching at all."

"I only tried to help the birds and wanted to see them up close," argued Sahil.

"In doing so, you scared them. Their parents felt **THREATENED** and therefore tried to attack you," explained Uncle Dinesh.

"Uncle, I do love birds and want to learn more. How can I do this without scaring them?" asked Sahil.

"You can observe them in their natural habitat from a distance. If you do that regularly, you will learn more about them. That is what birdwatchers do," said Uncle Dinesh.

"Won't I have to go to a bird sanctuary for that?" Sahil asked.

"Our garden and the park nearby are wonderful places to start. They are home to a variety of plants and trees. Birds visit such places for food and to build nests," said Uncle Dinesh.

"Uncle, how do you know so much about birds?" asked Sahil. "I am a birdwatcher, Sahil. I observe them and prepare notes.

When we do that, not only do we understand a bird's behaviour, nesting habits and sounds, but it brings us closer to nature," said Uncle Dinesh.

"What is the use of making notes, Uncle Dinesh?"

"**ORNITHOLOGISTS** benefit from it too. Our neighbour, Dr. Shyam is an Ornithologist and my observations help him. We meet quite often and discuss our observations and findings," said Uncle Dinesh.

Studying Birds

"Who is an Ornithologist, Uncle?" asked Sahil.

"A person who studies birds as a science, is called an Ornithologist," explained Uncle Dinesh.

"You study birds, too. So, are you an Ornithologist?"

"Ha ha! No, Sahil. **ORNITHOLOGY** is a branch of science and is formally taught in some colleges. I am a hobbyist birdwatcher," said Uncle Dinesh.

"Then why does Uncle Shyam take your advice?" asked Sahil. "Daily observations from hobbyist birdwatchers like me can give Ornithologists key information like bird population in a specific area, or changes in their behavioural patterns. Also when Uncle Shyam travels, he needs someone to observe the birds here. That's where my observations come in handy," said Uncle Dinesh.

Binoculars and Bulbuls

Uncle Dinesh led Sahil to the terrace. "Now observe the birds for as long as you wish," he said, handing him a pair of **binoculars**.

Sahil began to look for birds through the binoculars and almost immediately **SQUEALED** with excitement. "I just spotted a bulbul with a lovely crest on its head!" he exclaimed, pointing towards a large tree.

"I spot a second bulbul near it. Their nest must be close by," said Uncle Dinesh. "Yes! Their nest is cleverly hidden between the branches of that tree. I can see three eggs in it," said Sahil, adjusting the **ZOOM** on his binoculars. From that day on, Sahil observed the pair of bulbuls every day and even wrote

notes. He was amazed to see the eggs **hatch** and tiny chicks emerge. They grew into plump birds that chattered non-stop. Their wings grew stronger and they flew away from their nest. Sahil was sad to see the empty nest. But his interest was immediately caught by a chatty pair of mynahs on the Gulmohar tree!

Sahil **JOTTED** down whatever observations he made and shared them with his family, friends, teachers and of course, Uncle Dinesh. He made a project for his school on birdwatching as a hobby, which won him the first prize.

"You have become a bird expert," his friends said.

"Not yet," Sahil replied, "But if I keep working on it and study hard, I can definitely become an Ornithologist one day!"

Blowing To and Fro
By Vandana Gupta

Winnie wind was quite naughty. She liked to play tricks on everyone. That day, she was in the mood for some **MISCHIEVOUS** fun.

"I will blow around really hard and work up a storm! Everyone will be troubled," she decided.

No sooner had she started WHIRLING upwards than she noticed a rather large balloon in the air.

"What is such a huge balloon doing so high up in the air," she thought and hailed the balloon, "Hey, what are you doing up here?"

"I am a weather balloon," it replied, "Weather scientists have sent me up here."

"How did they do that?"

"They filled me with hydrogen, which makes me fly 30 to 40 kilometres up into the air. Another gas called helium also has this effect on me."

The Balloon plays Spoilsport

"Why did they send you here, though?" Winnie was curious.
"To record weather updates."

"How can a balloon understand the weather?" Winnie smirked.

"You see the a black box tied to me? It is a machine with several functions, which connect me to the weather department. It can record my location, temperature, speed of the wind, **HUMIDITY** and much more."

"The Scientists down there track my location, and the recorded data helps them calculate the weather. They find out about an approaching **THUNDERSTORM** or bad weather through this data and alert everyone before it occurs."

"Will you float around like this forever?" Winnie was annoyed at the prospect. "I'm afraid not," the balloon replied. "At first, my diameter was only two metres. However it kept increasing as I rose higher. When my **diameter** increases 20 to 30 times, I will burst and the small box tied to me will drop down. The scientists will pick it up and retrieve data from it," the weather balloon said.

Winnie was deep in thought, "What is the use of **KICKING** up a storm if everyone gets warned about it in advance? They will all remain indoors and no-one will get scared," she wondered.

Right then, an idea occurred to her. "Why don't I try my plan over the ocean? I will blow on the water rapidly and whip up a really good storm. That will certainly cause trouble for everyone!"

Change of Plans

Winnie bid the weather balloon goodbye and moved towards the ocean. There, she noticed a small boat full of **whirring** machines of all sorts. There was nobody on the boat and it was floating around on its own.

"Who are you, and what are you doing here?" Winnie asked.

"I am a buoy. I warn weather scientists about the time and **location** of upcoming storms."

"You too!?" Winnie exclaimed.

"I can also give them **READINGS** about the surface of the ocean. I tell them the temperature and the speed of the

water beneath and alert them if a storm is about to set in. They then warn ships and fishermen to stay away from the ocean if that is the case." "The weather department has deployed its spies everywhere!" Winnie was feeling a bit stormy herself, "I can't work my MISCHIEF here either!"

As a last resort, she decided to enlist the help of the clouds.

"I'll push all the water-filled clouds into one place," Winnie decided. "They will rub against each other, become **ELECTRICALLY CHARGED** and create lightning, thunder and rain. I will then blow very hard and make scary, swooshing noises. People will be TERRIFIED."

A Pleasant Breeze

Winnie made her way to the clouds and asked them to co-**OPERATE** with her plan. The clouds laughed and said, "There's no point in doing all of that! Some time ago, a **radar** came up here and measured us. It must have informed the scientists by now. They already know where we are and how much we weigh." "How is that possible? There are no machines near you," Winnie refused to believe them.

"Radars **EMIT** waves that travel through air and reach us. They bounce back to the radar and the scientists calculate the time and speed of these returning waves. They find out everything about where we are, how heavy we are, and when and where we would cause rainfall," the clouds explained.

"There goes my lastidea: create trouble and have fun!" Winnie felt **deflated**.

"The scientists keep a tab on everything, Winnie. Every country has weather-reading equipment all over the **atmosphere**. They are in close contact with each other, and share knowledge between themselves. Together, they work out where it might rain, what the temperature is likely to be, and where a storm might take place. The public is warned via television, newspapers, radio and **mobile apps** so people can be prepared and keep themselves safe," the clouds concluded. Winnie was tired of trying to hatch pranks and began moving to and fro in a park, lost in thought. After a few minutes, she overheard some people talking, "Even on such a hot day, there is a lovely cool **breeze** here. Such nice weather!"

"I wanted to disturb everyone. Instead, I ended up helping them just by slowing down and moving to and fro," Winnie realised, "Perhaps it is a better idea to help people than to trouble them!"

The Cat in the Computer

By Indrajit Kaushik

"Come here, son! I want to show you this book I found," Dhanush's father called out to him.

Dhanush was in the garden, playing with a ball. Leaving the game, he ran into the house. In the same garden was a burrow and in it lived Montu **mouse** with his mother Manjula mouse. Montu loved books, and upon overhearing the conversation, followed Dhanush into the house. Dhanush sat on his father's lap and Montu found a nice spot behind them where he was well-hidden and could see the book too.

"See Dhanush, this is an **ALPHABET** book. It has words and pictures in it. A is for apple, B is for boy," Dhanush's father read out while showing him the book.

Both Dhanush and Montu were excited. Dhanush flipped the pages and stopped at one.

"What is this, Papa?" he asked, pointing to a picture in the book. "That looks exactly like me!" thought Montu as he looked at the picture. "That is a mouse," explained Dhanush's father. "It starts with the letter M.".

"Mouse! So that's what humans call me! I like that word," thought Montu.

Hunger leads to a Friend

Dhanush finished reading the book and went outside to play. Dhanush's father went to the study room to teach Dhanush's sister Pinky how to operate the computer. Montu was starting to get hungry and decided to look for some food. In the study room, Pinky was **DISINTERESTED** in what her father was trying to teach her. "Pinky, stop getting distracted and pay attention. Come on, hold the mouse properly," he said firmly.

Montu was nearby and heard what father was saying. "Oh no! Have they caught a mouse? Are they going to catch me next?" he wondered and ran for safety. Several hours passed and with no sign of anybody trying to hunt for him, Montu decided to peep out of his hiding place. He hadn't eaten all day and his **TUMMY** was **RUMBLING** When he stepped out and began to look for food, Montu realised that everybody in the house must have gone to sleep.

He went to the kitchen and found the door locked.
DEJECTED, he wandered around the house in search of food and wound up in the study room, where the computer was set up.

Montu went up to the computer table and climbed on to it. He looked at the **MONITOR**, the **keyboard** and saw a strange thing on the desk which almost looked like a mouse, but wasn't one.

"Hello," said the computer mouse, welcoming Montu.

"Hi, you look just like me. What is your name?" Montu asked the computer mouse.

"I'm a mouse. Nice to meet you. May I know your name?" asked the computer mouse.

"My name is Montu, and I'm a mouse, too. I read it in a book just some time ago," said Montu.

"That explains it. I was wondering why humans call me a mouse. It's because I look a lot like you!" said the computer mouse.

"Do you want to go find some food with me?" Montu asked the computer mouse.

"I'd love to, Montu, but unlike you, I don't need to eat food. Also, I'm connected to the computer with this wire. I can't travel very far," said the computer mouse. "Don't worry, I'll take care of that," said Montu and **CHEWED** through the mouse's cable with his teeth. The moment the cable was cut, the computer mouse stopped talking. The next morning, Pinky's father noticed that the mouse wasn't working and replaced the cable.

Montu gets a Scare

That night, Montu went back to meet his new friend. "What happened to you yesterday?" he asked the computer mouse. "I tried to tell you, but you didn't give me a chance. I'm afraid I can't go anywhere with you. I need to be **CONNECTED** to the computer to stay alive," said the computer mouse.

Montu felt bad at first, but then realised that he could always play with the computer mouse here in the house. With a smile, he asked the computer mouse whether it could teach him how to operate the computer.

"Sure, let's try," said the computer mouse. "First, I want you to click the **button** on my left side."

Montu looked around to see if there was anybody watching them. "Oh! You were talking to me? I didn't understand a word of what you just said," said Montu. With a laugh, the computer mouse explained that it had two buttons, one at its top-left side and the other at the top-right. It also taught Montu how to use the buttons. When Montu pushed down on the computer mouse's left button, the computer booted up and a picture appeared. It was the computer's wallpaper.

"Oh no! That's a cat!" shouted Montu and began **SCRAMBLING** away.

"It's not a real cat! It's only a **wallpaper**," said the computer mouse, but Montu had already run away.

Once Montu was safely back in his **BURROW** in the garden, he told his mother Manjula mouse what had just happened.

"Dearest Montu," she said. "If the cat was inside the computer, then it means it's not real!"

"Well, I knew that! But what if the cat came alive and jumped out?" asked Montu.

Manjula mouse laughed and went back to doing her chores.

ANSWERS

PAGE 123: HIDDEN PICTURE

PAGE 131: SCHOOL SEARCH

PAGE 78: BACK TO SCHOOL

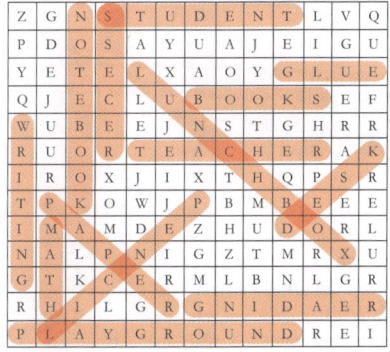

PAGE 36: SOLVE IT

Whales eat - 7 X 5 = 35 stalks
Manta Rays eat - 6 X 1 = 6 stalks
Small fish eat - 16 X 1/4 = 4 stalks
Total - 46 stalks of seaweed grow there everyday.

PAGE 15: SOLVE IT

1. Today was the first day of school. I got dressed quickly and ran all the way there, where I met Meeku and Jumbo. I climbed up on Jumbo to see if we would all be in the same class.

2. Yes! Meeku, Jumbo and I were together. Our first subject was History and we went to class.

3. After attendance was taken, our teacher wanted to know what we did in our vacations. When it was my turn, I told the teacher how I learned to swim.

4. After school, I said bye to my friends and returned home.

More in the Series

Experience the excitement of Laxman and Hari, who become teachers, only to realise how chaotic classrooms can be. Root for Ritwik, who faces and overcomes name-calling at school. Feel the exam-time jitters that push Riya into a sticky situation, or read how Nitya adapts to a new school in a new city over a shared lunch. Have fun with Mittu's mother, who makes him love school with a clever plan and chuckle when friends Ritesh and Abhay go silent on stage in a monologue competition!

Packed with action and emotions, *Champak School-Day Stories* is a must-have collection of the ups and downs, the hits and misses, and the topsy-turvy days of school life.